DOCTOR WHO
THE VISITATION

THE CHANGING FACE OF DOCTOR WHO
The cover illustration portrays the Fifth Doctor whose
physical appearance later changed after his body was
infected with spectrox toxaemia.

Also available from BBC Books:

DOCTOR WHO

THE VISITATION

Based on the BBC Television serial *The Visitation*
by Eric Saward by arrangement with the BBC

ERIC SAWARD

BOOKS

1 3 5 7 9 10 8 6 4 2

BBC Books, an imprint of Ebury Publishing
20 Vauxhall Bridge Road,
London SW1V 2SA

BBC Books is part of the Penguin Random House group of companies
whose addresses can be found at global.penguinrandomhouse.com

Published by BBC Books in 2016
First published in 1982 by Universal-Tandem Publishing Co. Ltd.

www.eburypublishing.co.uk

A CIP catalogue record for this book is available from the British Library

ISBN 978 1 785 94039 2

Editorial Director: Albert DePetrillo
Editorial Manager: Grace Paul
Series Consultant: Justin Richards
Cover design: Lee Binding © Woodlands Books Ltd, 2016
Cover illustration: Chris Achilleos
Production: Alex Goddard

Printed and bound in the U.S.A.

Typeset in India by Thomson Digital Pvt Ltd, Noida, Delhi

Contents

The Changing Face of Doctor Who

The Fifth Doctor

This *Doctor Who* novel features the fifth incarnation of the Doctor. In this incarnation the Doctor was perhaps at his most 'human'. The Fifth Doctor was apparently younger than his predecessors. But despite his apparent youth, the Doctor demonstrates again and again a depth of wisdom and experience that is at odds with his appearance.

The Fifth Doctor was also more affected by the process of regeneration, needing to spend time in the TARDIS Zero Room in order to recover from the experience.

Rather than a father figure, he was more of an older brother to his companions, and his affection for them was obvious. He is also perhaps the most selfless of the Doctor's incarnations. Ultimately, he sacrifices his own life to save Peri Brown – a young woman he barely knows.

Adric

A talented mathematician, Adric comes from a community stranded on the planet Alzarius. He hid on board the TARDIS after the Doctor, Romana and K-9 helped his people repair their Starliner and leave the planet.

Socially inept, and rather selfish, Adric does mellow during his time on board the TARDIS. He gradually comes to appreciate and care for other people, although he is never one to philosophise or suffer from a moral dilemma. Throughout his time in the TARDIS, Adric tends to put himself first. This attitude is exaggerated by contrast with the selfless Nyssa, but tempered by his growing admiration for the Doctor.

Nyssa

Nyssa joins the Doctor after her father is killed by the Master (who steals his body for himself) and her own world, Traken, is destroyed by an entropy cloud.

During her travels, Nyssa is frequently frustrated at the lack of opportunity to put her considerable technical skills to good use. There are occasions where they come in useful, but for the most part, Nyssa feels under-employed on the TARDIS. She is not one to complain, however, always putting others before herself, perhaps because she has lost so much.

Tegan

An impulsive, self-confident Australian woman, Tegan is on her way to her first day at work as an air stewardess when she finds the TARDIS. She realises at once that it is a vehicle, and she implicitly trusts the Doctor.

Despite being inclined to be rather bossy, Tegan and Nyssa become friends – although she finds Adric rather irritating. While she enjoys her time in the TARDIS, Tegan is initially keen to get back to Heathrow and her job. She is constantly – and vocally – frustrated by the Doctor's apparent inability to get her there.

Chapter 1

It was a warm summer evening. The rays of the setting sun bathed the old manor house in subtle shades of red and gold. Evening stars appeared as the light continued to fade. From a high branch, a sleepy owl watched a fox break cover and silently pad towards the west wing of the manor house.

Night was awakening. Small furry animals with bright, shiny eyes scurried through the undergrowth in search of food. A grass snake, warm and refreshed from a day spent lying in the sun, tentatively flexed his body and explored the air with a series of short, sharp, flicking movements of his highly sensitive tongue. The owl, now fully awake, stared fixedly, saucer-eyed, at a shadow below. Suddenly he launched himself into space, and on silent wings, talons extended, sped towards a tiny harvest mouse. A moment later, the bird's hooked beak was tearing at his supper. It was the first kill of the evening.

With her day book before her on the window seat of her bedroom, Elizabeth watched the fox as he trotted by below. Smiling, she picked up her quill, dipped it into her pewter ink pot and recorded the sighting in her best copperplate hand-writing. She then replenished her quill, and, at the bottom of the entry, set its creaking, scratchy nib to uncoil, in black ink, the date: 5th August 1666. Blotting the sheet carefully, she closed the day book, rose, picked up the candle and crossed to the door.

With long skirts carefully controlled, Elizabeth started to negotiate the steep, narrow stairs from her bedroom. As she descended she heard the distant bark of the fox. Hoping to catch a last glimpse, she paused at the stairway's tiny lancet window and peered out. But the only moving thing visible was what appeared to be a ball of light slowly crossing the sky. Elizabeth stared at the object, puzzled by its slowness and the acute angle at which it was travelling towards Earth. If it was a shooting star, she thought, it was unlike any she had seen before.

Surprise replaced puzzlement when, at great speed, a tiny but very distinct bolt of light was ejected from the main ball. Elizabeth watched as the bolt not only rapidly decelerated, but also lost light intensity. A moment later the main ball exploded, creating a pyrotechnic display of such magnificence, it looked as though a million fireworks had been ignited at the same moment. Overcome with excitement, Elizabeth half ran, half fell down the remaining stairs.

In the main hall of the house, Sir John dozed before the unlit fireplace. He had just consumed a vast meal along with two bottles of his favourite wine. Although the rhythmic movement of his bulky stomach suggested contentment, his high colour and twitching countenance more accurately indicated the onset of indigestion.

Ralph, the elderly servant, blew out the taper he had been using to light extra candles, and slipped it behind his ear for safe keeping. 'Do you want me to clear away, Master Charles?' he said.

Charles, who was sitting in his favourite chair cleaning a pair of saddle pistols, glanced across at his now-snoring father. 'Leave the bread and cheese,' he said, 'I'm sure Sir John will want a little more to eat before retiring.' He gazed at the undulating stomach and sighed. 'Although heaven only knows where he puts it all.'

The servant smiled and started to shuffle towards the dining table. Suddenly the door burst open and the highly excited Elizabeth rushed into the room. 'Papa! Papa!'

Sir John's face turned deep purple as he coughed, spluttered and then sat bolt upright, placing his hand on his racing heart. 'Fire and brimstone!' he screamed. 'You should know better than to enter a room like that.'

'I am sorry, Papa,' she bubbled, setting her candle on a side table and running to the window, 'but you must see them.'

Sir John craned his neck as he endeavoured to keep his daughter in view.

'The lights, Papa.' She tugged at the curtains. 'They're so beautiful.'

'Lights?' Sir John clambered awkwardly out of his chair. 'What lights?' It was clear he was uneasy.

Elizabeth continued her tussle with the drapes, but her final victory was a hollow one. 'Oh, they've gone,' she sighed, staring into the blackness of the night.

Sir John turned from the window, clearly disturbed. 'What were the lights like?' he muttered.

'Like a million shooting stars. The whole sky was ablaze.'

The old knight made his way to the dining table, picked up a quarter-full bottle of wine and emptied it into a goblet. Charles watched, concerned by his father's reaction. 'Are you all right, father?'

'Of course I'm all right,' he growled. 'It's just this talk of lights.' He paused, staring into the goblet. 'I don't like the sound of it.'

Elizabeth moved to her father's side. 'Oh, Papa.' Her tone was slightly disapproving of his superstitious response.

'Strange lights do not bode well for the future. Take my word.'

Elizabeth reached up and kissed her father affectionately on the cheek. 'You're so sweet.' The old man snorted. 'You're so sweet... and so old-fashioned,' she laughed.

Sir John took a long swallow from his goblet and then looked down at his smiling daughter.

'Maybe you're right,' he said at last. 'Maybe you're right.' But in his heart he was less certain.

The fox Elizabeth had watched earlier with such pleasure continued his nightly patrol. Now clear of the house, he raced across the open ground to the high brick perimeter-wall of the estate. He paused to sniff the air. Something was wrong.

Undeterred, he made his way along the wall until he came to a small gate. Without hesitation he squeezed through its narrow bars. Ahead lay the forest and a good night's hunting. But something was definitely wrong.

Cautiously, the fox moved into the silent forest, ears cocked, nose keenly analysing the night air. He sensed danger. The game keeper? The local poacher? But no. He knew their smells only too well. This was new. Something was burning.

The fox moved on. Thin, whispy twirls of smoke hung in the air and bushes, its acrid smell irritating his nose and eyes. He sneezed hard and shook his head, trying to clear the irritation. A little way ahead he noticed an enormous, dark shape surrounded by flattened, smouldering undergrowth.

Frantically he tried to make sense of the silhouette. Then the shape seemed slowly to split open, purple light pouring from the crack. This was too much for the poor old fox, who panicked and fled into the night.

As the split grew larger, an open hatchway could be seen behind what was now clearly a ramp being lowered. As it descended, a figure appeared, his massive form dividing the flood of purple light and casting an enormous shadow across the forest.

When the ramp was fully lowered, he began to move. Wheezing and gasping, his lungs unaccustomed to the Earth's thin atmosphere, he lumbered down the ramp and across the charred undergrowth. He paused for a moment, sniffing the air in much the same way the fox had. He then let out a loud hiss, turned and started towards the manor house.

*

By the light of a large candelabra Elizabeth and her father were playing cards. Sir John had always fancied himself a good card-player. Indeed he was, as his winnings far exceeded his losses. But Elizabeth, his pretty, shy, excitable daughter was better; much better. Her fast, nimble mind quickly grasped her opponent's stratagems. She had an excellent memory and could always remember which cards had already been played. Reluctantly her father had acknowledged her superior skill, but it still irked him to lose.

Shoulders hunched, lips pursed in concentration, Sir John watched his daughter pick up a card from the pack face-down on the table. Impassively, she slotted it into those she already held, barely pausing before discarding an unwanted card. Sir John glanced down at the neatly fanned cards in his hand and smiled. She had thrown away the very card he wanted. The game is mine, he thought, reaching for it.

'Too late, Papa.' Elizabeth placed her own cards on the table. 'I think I've won.' Sir John scanned them with piggy eyes hoping for a mistake. But no, she had won again.

Charles laughed, 'Well done, sister!'

The old knight scowled as he gathered the cards together.

'Luck,' he muttered, 'pure luck.'

'Be fair, father. You were beaten by the better player.'

'My concentration was spoiled,' he growled, as Ralph entered the room. 'I could feel a chill on my neck.'

'Impossible, Papa. It's a perfectly warm evening.'

Charles pushed his chair back from the card table, making a harsh, rasping noise on the flagstone floor, and stood up. 'Father always feels a chill when he's losing,' he said, crossing to where he had left his pistols. 'It's either that or his gout bothers him.'

'Arrant nonsense. I felt a definite chill about my neck and shoulders.'

The large candelabra flickered as though to prove his point. 'You see!' Sir John crowed.

'Perhaps Ralph should fetch your shawl, Papa.'

Sir John frowned. He hated his shawl. To him it was the mark of an old man. Years may have aged his body, but not his spirit. 'Certainly not,' he said, clearing his throat, 'I'll have a warmer. Fetch me a posset, Ralph.'

Charles glared at his father as he picked up the pistols. 'You are incorrigible. Haven't you drunk enough already?'

Sir John started to shuffle the cards. He had anticipated disapproval. 'This is medicinal,' he snapped. 'It helps keep the cold out.'

'Cold? We've barely scratched August, yet your consumption of this "medicine" suggests we are but half a day from the winter solstice.'

Sir John grunted. But before he could think of an answer, Charles had marched out of the room.

'Insolent oaf!'

Pretending to be bothered by an itch, but really to hide the fact she was smiling, Elizabeth rubbed her nose with the flat of her hand. 'I think I should retire, too, Papa.'

'You remain seated,' he grumbled, starting to deal. 'I've brooked enough humiliation from my offspring for one evening. We will play one more game. And this time I shall win.'

Elizabeth picked up the cards he had dealt her and fanned them out. 'You can certainly try, Papa,' she said, and smiled sweetly.

On the landing outside the main hall where the card game was still in progress, Charles stood before the heavy, oak gun cupboard, rummaging in his pocket for the key. As he searched, Ralph appeared carrying two candles.

'I thought you might need this, Master Charles.' Gratefully Charles took one of the candles and placed it on the floor near the cupboard.

Finally locating the key, Charles inserted it in the lock, but the lock was stiff and he had great difficulty in operating it.

'I think a little rendered sheep fat would work miracles,' said the old retainer, shuffling across the landing. 'I'll attend to it tomorrow.'

Just then the lock gave and, creaking loudly, the cupboard swung open to reveal a row of muskets.

'I take it you're not having a posset, Master Charles.'

'No, thank you.'

'Then I'll wish you good night.'

'Good night.'

The servant descended the back stairs and entered the passage that led to the kitchen, his feet making a crunching sound on the straw-covered floor.

Gradually he became aware that he was not alone. Ahead he could hear a low, hissing wheeze, which sounded like someone struggling for breath.

He stopped and held out his candle, but the light didn't spread far enough into the darkness for him to see who or what it was. 'Who's there?' he said uncertainly. 'I can hear you.' But there was no reply. Instead the hissing grew louder as it moved closer.

Ralph began to back down the passage, his nervous fingers easing the candle from its heavy base. Suddenly there was a loud roar. Ralph screamed and hurled the candlestick into the dark, before turning and fleeing back along the passage.

Heart pounding, leg muscles heavy with fear, the old man ran as fast as he could. As he emerged from the passage, he saw Charles running down the stairs. 'Fetch a pistol, Master Charles. There's some...' But before he could finish the sentence, a loud whining noise was heard as a narrow pencil-beam of green light shot from the tunnel, striking Ralph in the back. The old servant screamed as he collapsed, his candle rolling across the floor.

Horrified, Charles turned and rushed up the stairs to the armoury cupboard. Flinging open the unlocked doors, he snatched up a pistol and started to prime it, his eyes constantly darting between the weapon and the stairs.

With the gun loaded, Charles poured a little powder into the flash pan. As he was doing this, he became aware of a massive figure standing at the foot of the stairs.

'Who's there?' Charles called. 'I'll shoot if you don't reply.'

Like a death rattle, the whining sound was heard again and the thin beam of green light exploded against the baluster in front of him.

Charles fired his pistol. The huge creature roared in pain and collapsed, his leg shattered.

Quickly Charles reloaded his pistol as the main door was flung open and Sir John rushed onto the landing. 'Fire and brimstone!' he screamed. 'And what do you think you are doing, sir?'

Charles thrust a pistol into his father's hand. 'Load this,' he said urgently. 'There's something down there with a gun the likes of which I've never seen before.'

Sir John did as instructed. 'Where's Ralph?'

'I fear he's hit.' And as Charles spoke, another beam of light was fired, this time striking the armoury cupboard. 'Look!' he shouted.

The strange creature was dragging his massive form across the floor to the passage leading to the kitchen.

With weapons loaded, both men fired. The creature roared and screamed, then rolled onto his back. In the darkness, thin yellow fluid spurted from his wounds.

'What was it?' Sir John whispered in a voice hoarse with fear.

Before Charles could comment, they heard a hammering and splintering of wood coming from the direction of the great hall.

'Father! Charles! Quick!' shouted a terrified Elizabeth.

Grabbing muskets and ammunition, Sir John and Charles ran to join Elizabeth. They could hear the heavy front door being torn from its hinges.

'What's happening, Papa?'

'Would it be too obvious to say we were under attack?'

'But from whom?'

There were heavy, metallic footsteps in the hallway.

'From whatever that thing is,' muttered Sir John.

Charles handed his sister a musket and quickly the family loaded their weapons. This was no sooner done than the door of the room was flung open. The trio cocked their muskets. Standing in the doorway was what appeared to be a man in a steel suit.

'This one's wearing armour.'

'Our shot stopped his comrade on the stairs, father. And armour at this range is useless.' Charles raised his musket. 'Come on,' he shouted.

Elizabeth and Sir John also levelled their weapons. The intruder remained impassive as three ear-splitting shots were fired at him. Then slowly the steel shape raised a finger in an accusatorial manner, and several bolts of light were hurled against the horrified trio.

A moment later, all that remained of the family were three charred, smoking bodies.

Chapter 2

Aboard the TARDIS, Nyssa watched as Tegan, the Doctor's air-hostess companion, packed her few belongings into a shoulder-bag. She was going home, back to her own time. At least, that's what the Doctor had promised.

Carefully Tegan brushed smooth the wrinkled cover of her bed.

'I won't be sleeping here again,' she said sadly, looking round the room she had shared with Nyssa for what seemed like an age. Its mixture of Art Deco and Victorian furnishings had never really pleased her, but now she was going she would quite miss it.

'I know I've made so much fuss about going home...' She was unable to finish the sentence. She swallowed hard and wiped away a tear. 'I'm being silly.'

'Of course you're not.' Nyssa picked up Tegan's uniform jacket and helped her put it on. 'You'll soon settle down.'

'I hope so. It's going to be pretty unbearable if I don't.' With her jacket fastened, Tegan fumbled with the catch on her bag, more for something to do with her hands than to check if it was secure.

'At least you won't have any awkward questions to answer about where you've been.'

'So the Doctor said.' Tegan picked up her bag and followed Nyssa out of the room. 'But I don't understand how.'

'Such is time travel. You'll arrive at the airport exactly on time for the flight you were supposed to catch. And as though nothing had happened.'

'Tell that to Aunt Vanessa,' Tegan muttered, remembering how her favourite relation had been murdered by the Master during that fateful journey to Heathrow.

'I'm sorry,' said Nyssa, 'I'd forgotten.'

Tegan smiled weakly. 'It's me who should apologise.' Tears welled up in her eyes again. 'I know I haven't been the best of companions, but I'm going to miss you... all of you.' The two women hugged each other.

'We'll miss you, too, Tegan.'

The Doctor stood before the console, the time rotor now stationary.

'Earth,' he said confidently. 'Heathrow 1981. Not one of the most stimulating places in the Universe.

But, nevertheless, where requested to be.' The Doctor pressed a button on the console, and the shield covering the scanner-screen rose. Adric, who had been busily working on some calculations, had not heard the Doctor's remark. It was the Time Lord's groan of despair that broke into his thought.

Adric looked up and then glanced across at the screen. Instead of Heathrow Airport there were trees–a whole forest full.

'I've done it again,' the Doctor moaned, and at that very moment Tegan entered the console room. Attempting to hide his blunder, the Doctor fumbled with the scanner-screen control, but he was too late.

'Is that supposed to be Heathrow?' she shouted, a rigid finger pointing at the screen.

'It is,' said Adric firmly.

'Well, they've let the grass grow since I was last here.'

'Actually, they haven't built the airport yet,' Adric continued. 'We're about three hundred years early.'

'That's great! Perhaps I should slip outside and file a claim on the land. When they get around to inventing the aeroplane, I'll make a fortune!'

The Doctor tried to explain what had gone wrong with the TARDIS, but Tegan was too angry to listen. Instead she stormed over to the console and operated the door-opening mechanism. 'Call yourself a Time

Lord,' she shouted. 'A broken clock keeps better time than you. At least it's right twice a day, which is more than you are!' That said, she stalked out of the TARDIS.

The Doctor fumed for a moment. 'How dare she talk to me like that!'

Nyssa, who had heard them arguing as she came down the corridor, tried to pacify the Doctor. 'I think she's finding the idea of going more painful than she thought.'

'Then why didn't she say so?'

Nyssa shrugged. 'That's Tegan. Perhaps you should talk to her.'

The Doctor looked at Adric hoping for support, but his expression seemed to echo Nyssa's words. 'Oh, all right,' he said at last, 'I'll apologise.' Reluctantly he picked up his hat. 'But this is the last time,' he muttered as he left the TARDIS.

Pleased with their success as arbitrators, Nyssa and Adric exchanged a smile before following him.

The wood outside was warm and sunny. Tegan brushed a tear from her eye as the Doctor approached. Nyssa and Adric had decided to maintain a discreet distance. Apologising was something best done alone.

'I'm sorry,' the Doctor said awkwardly. 'I realise how disappointed you must be.'

Tegan turned towards the Doctor. 'I'm sorry, too. But you did promise to take me back to my own time.'

'And so I shall.' The Doctor snapped a twig from a low-hanging branch. 'But try and consider this a fortunate mistake.' And using the twig as a pointer, he indicated the wood about them. 'It isn't everyone who has a chance to wander about their own history.'

Tegan looked around. 'True. But I don't think I want to. This place stinks.'

'What?' The Doctor's hackles began to rise again. Then the foul smell hit him.

'Look, Doctor,' said Adric pointing at whisps of smoke hanging in the air.

The Doctor sniffed. 'Sulphur.'

'Some sort of volcanic action?'

'No, Adric. The wrong time and place for that.'

Tegan drove the heel of her shoe into the ground. 'Are you sure this is the planet Earth?'

'Undoubtedly.' He walked back to the TARDIS and closed its doors. 'If we find the person burning the sulphur, he'll tell you the same, and perhaps you'll believe him.'

Tegan frowned. 'I'm not sure I want to find whoever it is.' But the Doctor was already walking single-mindedly deeper into the forest. Tegan watched the intrepid explorer. 'I don't know why I bother to say anything,' she muttered, and reluctantly the Doctor's three companions followed him.

From high in a tree a masked man watched their progress as they stumbled along. Once they had passed by beneath him, he leaned out carefully from his perch and made four short staccato movements in the air with his club. The signal was acknowledged by another masked man similarly situated several hundred yards ahead of the Doctor's party.

The smoke grew denser as the little group walked even deeper into the forest.

'Do you think it wise to go on, Doctor?' said Nyssa anxiously.

'Probably not.' He sniffed the air. 'You know, there's potassium nitrate in with the sulphur. I can just smell it.'

'That's great!' said Tegan. 'All we need now is for you to say you can smell charcoal.'

'You're right. I hadn't thought of that.'

Puzzled, Nyssa looked at Adric. What are they talking about? her expression said. But Adric could only shrug his shoulders. 'Is there something wrong, Docter?' he asked.

'Charcoal, potassium nitrate and sulphur are constituents of a primitive explosive,' he said. 'It's known on Earth as gunpowder.'

'For all we know we could be very near to a place where they manufacture the stuff,' said Tegan nervously.

'I wonder.'

Through the smoke the outlines of three men carrying makeshift clubs could be seen hurrying towards them. The lower halves of their faces were covered in rough, sacking masks.

'They're footpads,' said Tegan quietly. 'I think it's time we returned to the TARDIS.'

They all agreed, but found, when they tried to turn back, their retreat cut off by two more armed men, clubs raised, charging towards them.

'What now?' said Adric. 'We can't fight all of them.'

'We bluff our way.' The Doctor stepped forward, smiling. 'Ah, good morning, gentlemen...' But before he could finish the first of the band was upon him, lashing out with his club. The Doctor ducked and weaved, trying every trick he knew to disarm him. But his attacker was no stranger to hand-to-hand fighting.

As the second man closed in, Adric ran behind him, dropped to the ground and made himself into a tight ball.

'Now!' shouted Tegan, and both she and Nyssa shoulder-charged the man, sending him tumbling backwards over Adric's crouched body.

The Doctor fought on, his opponent beginning to tire. The man lunged again, but this time the Doctor was able to side-step the blow and grab his attacker's tunic. The Doctor pulled hard, at the same moment

21

extending his leg, causing the bewildered man to trip and crash to the ground.

'Hurry, Doctor,' shouted Tegan. 'The others will be here in a moment.'

They ran off leaving their two attackers bewildered and winded. They ran as fast as they could, low branches of trees grabbing and whipping at them as they went. They ran until their lungs ached. Suddenly Adric fell to the ground, his foot twisted in a hole.

The others stopped while the Doctor bent down to feel Adric's leg for broken bones. Tegan remained on guard, watching for the three pursuers.

'Hurry, Doctor,' she shouted. 'I can see them. They're still following.'

'Come on,' grunted the Doctor as he pulled Adric to his feet. 'I'll help you.' But Adric couldn't place any weight on the damaged ankle. 'We must carry him,' the Doctor said urgently.

'I'll be all right in a minute.'

'We don't have a minute!' shouted Tegan.

'Then leave me.' Adric pulled himself free of the Doctor's grip and collapsed. 'Save yourselves.'

Tegan and Nyssa were beginning to panic as the three men drew nearer. 'We can't leave Adric,' said Tegan. 'They'll kill him.'

'I think not,' said a rich, plummy voice from above them.

Startled, they looked up and saw the portly frame of a man in his forties lounging on the limb of a tree. 'May I be of any assistance?'

'You think you can help us?' said the Doctor.

The stranger fingered the handles of two flintlock pistols protruding from a shabby sash at his middle. 'Indeed I can. I also have a convenient refuge nearby where the boy can rest.'

Tegan turned to the Doctor. 'How do we know we can trust him?'

'You have little choice.' The man removed his pistols and cocked them. 'You either trust me, or you give yourselves up to your pursuers...' He took careful aim. '...who would promptly cudgel you to death.' The guns exploded, causing a dozen pigeons to take flight and the three pursuers to dive for cover. 'Bull's-eye!'

'But you missed,' said Tegan.

'My intention was to scare, not maim.'

With considerably more flamboyance than the situation demanded, their unexpected rescuer thrust his pistols back into his waistband, adjusted a filthy dirty cravat at his neck, cocked his leg over the branch he was sitting on and slid to the ground.

'Richard Mace, ladies and gentlemen, at your service,' he said, and gave a small formal bow. 'If the boy can walk,' the portly man grunted, 'my camp is this way.'

Uncertain what to do, Tegan and Nyssa looked at the Doctor for guidance. 'Why not?' the Doctor said brightly, bending down to help Adric to his feet.

Tegan looked for the pursuers, but couldn't see them. 'Who were those people chasing us?' she said.

'Local villagers,' said Mace, striding off into the wood. 'I don't think they'll bother us any more.'

But he was mistaken. While one of the men returned to the village for help, the other two, very discreetly, continued to follow.

Chapter 3

Richard Mace pushed open the heavy door of the barn and bid the others enter.

The barn was cool and dry with a friendly smell.

In the loft, rats could be heard scampering about, while sunlight poured through a small window set high in one of the gable walls. Tegan wandered around the huge barn kicking the chaff on the floor, wondering why, as it was now early September, it only contained last year's debris and not this year's harvest.

'Is this home?'

'For the last night or two. Fortune has made me itinerant.'

'Why were those men chasing us?' asked the Doctor, completing his examination of Adric's leg.

'You really don't know?'

'We're new in the area.'

'You must be new to the world, sir.' Mace removed bread and cheese from a box normally used to store farm tools and started to attack the food with a knife. 'Haven't you heard? There is plague about.'

Tegan shuddered. 'Where?'

'Everywhere! That's why the village is guarded with such vigilance.' Mace cut a chunk of cheese from the wedge and offered it, with a thick slab of bread, to Nyssa. 'The villagers are terrified of strangers and the pestilence they might carry.'

'Of course!' exclaimed the Doctor. 'The reason for the sulphuric smoke: purification fires.'

'Is it because of the plague that you're not staying in the village?' said Tegan.

'Alas, the plague has made everywhere unfriendly.'

'Hence the guns?'

'Indeed.' Mace opened the wooden box and removed an earthenware jar. 'Once I was a noted thespian, until forced into rural exile by the closure of the theatres.' He struggled to remove the jar's stopper. 'Now it is only with the aid of pistols that I am able to command the attention of an audience.'

'You sound like a highwayman or robber,' said Tegan, instantly regretting her remark.

'Gentleman of the road, madam!' he said bowing. 'But do not be afraid. I only plan to rob you of a little time and company.'

Adric flexed his damaged leg. 'Aren't you concerned we may have plague?' he said as he pulled himself to his feet.

'After many weeks alone in the woods I am prepared to risk everything for an hour of good conversation.' Raising the jar to his lips, he swallowed several mouthfuls of wine. As he drank, tiny rivulets of red liquid trickled from either side of his mouth.

'Shouldn't we go, Doctor?' said Tegan.

'Soon,' he replied distractedly, staring at an ornament around the actor's neck. There was something familiar about it, but the Doctor couldn't quite remember what.

Mace set the jug down and returned to cutting up bread and cheese.

'How bad is the plague?' said Adric.

'The worst I've ever seen. Far more virulent in these parts than in the city.' He paused for a moment, then said quietly, 'I suppose that is to be expected.'

Tegan looked puzzled.

'Did you not see the comet a few weeks ago? A portent of doom if ever I saw one. Its aurora had barely faded from the sky when the first local case of the disease was reported.'

'That can't be possible,' the Doctor said vaguely, his mind only half concentrating on what was being said.

'Sir?'

'You're not due for a comet for...' he struggled to remember, '...well, at least, for quite some time.'

'Are you sure it wasn't a meteor?' said Nyssa.

'Call it by any name you wish, but I tell you the sky was lit as I've never seen it before.' He patted the jar of wine. 'And it had nothing to do with this.' Mace grunted. 'I have seen many falling stars. This one was without parallel.'

'Of course!' the Doctor said excitedly.

The others looked at him in surprise.

'What's the matter?' said Nyssa.

'Your necklace,' the Doctor said pointing at Mace, 'may I have a closer look?'

'If you wish.' Mace removed the ornament and handed it to the Doctor. 'But I hope you don't intend to lay claim to it,' he said a little stiffly.

The Doctor slipped on his half-frames. 'I shouldn't think so,' he said brightly, starting to examine it.

Mace felt uneasy. He watched for a moment as the Doctor scrutinised the object. 'I found it last night in the loft,' he said in an attempt to vindicate his ownership of the recently acquired possession.

The Doctor smiled. 'There's no doubt about it,' he said, handing the ornament to Nyssa.

Tegan looked worried. 'What's the matter?'

Nyssa dangled the object by its leather thong and flicked it with her finger.

28

'Well?' said Tegan, 'is no one going to answer me?'

'It's made from polygrite, isn't it?'

The Doctor nodded.

'But from such a primitive society?'

'Certainly not from this one.'

'Please, Doctor,' said Tegan becoming quite annoyed. 'What's going on?'

'First things first.' The Doctor crossed to the bottom of the loft ladder. 'You don't mind if I look up here, do you?'

Mace felt unnerved, but said, 'As you wish, sir.' However, he wasn't taking any chances. The small flourish of his hand, which seemed to endorse his agreement, casually petered out on the handle of one of his pistols.

The Doctor started to climb the ladder. 'Are you fit, Adric?' The boy flexed his leg and, barely limping now, crossed to the ladder.

'He ought to rest, Doctor,' Tegan protested.

But Adric had already started to climb. 'Don't worry, Tegan. We Alzarians are different. We heal much quicker than you.'

Mace smiled. He had pin-pointed his uneasiness about the Doctor and his friends. Foreigners, he thought, wondering where exactly Alzarians came from. At least that explained their strange costumes. He glanced at Tegan's knee-length skirt.

'Come on, Tegan. We can look around down here,' said Nyssa.

'And what are we looking for?' The air hostess was still annoyed as no one would tell her what was going on.

'Anything anachronistic.'

Tegan snorted. 'I assume that excludes us?'

The Doctor and Adric clambered into the loft and started to rummage among the thin layer of straw covering the floor.

'How could an ornament made of polygrite have got here, Doctor?'

'Make your own guess.' The Doctor coughed as dust wafted up from the disturbed straw. 'A comet that shouldn't be there, a meteor that doesn't look like a meteor–whatever the phenomenon was, it certainly wasn't natural.'

'A space craft landing?'

'Or burning up in the atmosphere.'

Adric straightened up. 'But for the ornament to be here, some of the crew must have survived.'

'Not necessarily. The ornament is hard enough to have endured the crash. But should we find something more delicate...'

'...then there are survivors,' said Adric.

'Right.'

30

'Doctor!' It was Nyssa. 'Is this what we're looking for?'

The Doctor leaned over the make-shift pole put up to act as a guard rail. Below, Nyssa stood with arm outstretched, the flat of her hand upwards. In her palm were three flat discs. 'Powerpacks,' she said proudly.

'Well done, Nyssa!' The Doctor bounced down the ladder to examine the find.

Richard Mace cleared his throat to attract the attention of these excitable foreigners. 'May I ask what is going on?'

'Questions later,' the Doctor said urgently. 'First, tell me, who owns this barn?'

Gravel crunched underfoot as the Doctor walked briskly up the driveway of the manor house, a highly agitated Richard Mace in tow.

Two masked villagers, still following the Doctor's party, reached the main gate of the drive just in time to see Tegan, Nyssa and Adric catching up with the irate actor and the Time Lord, who were now arguing heatedly. Bewildered, the two masked men concealed themselves behind the gate and observed their quarry, wondering what they were up to.

The Doctor increased his pace, but in spite of his heavy build Mace refused to be shaken off.

'Surely you are aware that there is a certain protocol involved when approaching the gentry?'

The Doctor didn't reply.

'Even if you are ignorant of that fact,' he continued to scream between loud rasping intakes of breath, 'you must realise that the nobility do not take kindly to being knocked up and questioned on the contents of their barn.'

'Then I will humour them,' the Doctor said over his shoulder.

'Sir, your humouring will earn all of us a horsewhipping. And I have a particularly sensitive skin!'

At last the actor's lungs gave out and he gently drifted to a halt in the middle of the drive.

'I thought highwaymen were bold and brave,' said Tegan.

'You forget, madam, I am also an actor. My bravado is as cracked as my wind.'

The Doctor continued on towards the house. As he approached the main door, a loaded wagon rounded the west corner at full gallop. Realising the danger, Tegan ushered Mace and the others off the driveway as the Doctor bolted for the porch of the house.

The wagon thundered along, its steel-rimmed wheels throwing up needle-sharp fragments of stone.

'Is the man blind?' screamed Nyssa, her hands raised to protect her head. 'He nearly killed us!'

As the wagon passed, Mace recognised the broad back and long grey hair of the man seated on the box. 'The Miller,' he said. 'A man of sour disposition.'

'Didn't he see us?' said Tegan.

'Who can...' But Mace didn't finish his sentence, the sound of fist upon wood interrupting his words. It was the Doctor beating on the main door of the house.

'No!' Mace shouted. 'You mustn't!' Invigorated by fear, Mace ran towards the house. 'Please don't,' he called. 'If you must knock, please let it be with more humility.'

The Doctor emerged from the porch and looked up at the red-brick facade and leaded windows. All was still. Even the chimney for the wood-burning stove in the kitchen was without smoke.

'Well, Doctor?' said Nyssa. 'What next?'

'I'm going to look around.'

Tegan sat down on the porch step and removed a shoe. 'Do you want us to come with you?' she said, rubbing her sore foot.

'Just Nyssa. I want you and Adric to keep knocking. Mr Mace will show you how it should be done.'

A sarcastic grunt was heard from the shadows of the porch. 'And what, pray, do you propose we say if the door is opened?'

33

' "Hullo" is the usual greeting.'

Mace lurched from the porch, but the Doctor and Nyssa had gone. 'I know these people,' he shouted after the Doctor. 'I know what they can be like.'

'I don't,' said Tegan sharply, 'and I never will, unless you can get one of them to open that door.'

Mace scowled. He was not happy.

Chapter 4

The Doctor and Nyssa made their way along the front of the house, pausing momentarily to peer in at the windows.

'Doctor? If there isn't anyone at home, then who was the miller visiting?'

They turned the west corner of the house.

'He could have been making a delivery.'

'Didn't you see his wagon? It was fully loaded.'

Pausing, the Doctor started to wipe the dust from a small leaded pane with the cuff of his jacket. 'Then he must have been collecting.'

'From whoever brought the polygrite to Earth?'

'Perhaps.'

The Doctor stared through the polished glass into the main hall of the house. Before the unlit fireplace stood Sir John's favourite chair. Nearby was the small table, playing cards spread across it as though hurriedly abandoned by the players. Lying next to the table, like dead sentries, were two stiff back chairs.

At the far end of the room was a long oak dining-table on which stood a large wedge of stale cheese, dark and cracked with age. Next to it was a loaf of bread covered with mildew.

The Doctor was about to continue making his way round the house, when he noticed that the window he was looking through wasn't fastened properly.

'Doctor! What are you doing?'

With the window open, the Doctor pulled himself up, and climbed in. 'Come on, Nyssa,' he said jumping down into the main hall. 'There isn't anyone here.' And before she could argue caution, he had gone.

Nyssa followed unenthusiastically. As she climbed through the window, she saw the Doctor moving methodically around the room.

'What precisely are we looking for?'

'Alien artefacts.'

'Why are you so worried about an alien landing? They might be friendly.' Nyssa jumped down from the sill.

'If I'm right,' the Doctor said, opening a large wooden linen-chest, 'the comet that Mace saw was their ship burning up. They're probably stranded here, desperate. They could wreak havoc.' Finding the chest empty, the Doctor closed it and idly ran his fingers over the lid, leaving a snail-like trail in the dust. 'It looks as though there hasn't been anyone here in weeks.'

'Perhaps they're on holiday?'

'It's the first of September, Nyssa. Harvest time. The busiest period of the year.'

'That doesn't mean the aliens have been here. For all we know, they could have gone to the village.'

'I know. They could also have died of plague. It's all guesswork. But as we're here, let's look a little further.'

The Doctor opened the door leading to the back landing and disappeared. Nyssa followed and found him squatting before the open armoury cupboard examining spilled gunpowder. 'Someone has been careless.'

But Nyssa wasn't listening. 'Look, Doctor,' she said, pointing at a hexagonal scar burnt deep into the baluster. 'That's been made by a high energy beam.'

The Doctor slipped on his half-frames and studied the mark. After a moment he said, 'It's been fired from a weapon.'

'So much for my friendly aliens.'

'Let's give them the benefit of the doubt and assume it was an accident...' But the Doctor's voice trailed off as his gaze wandered beyond the baluster and down the stairway. At the bottom was a brick wall.

He rose, quickly made his way down the stairs, and started to examine the wall. After a moment's thought,

he said, 'You only build a staircase to lead somewhere…
That being so, why should anyone build a wall here?'
He tapped the wall as a professor might a specimen
when emphasising a point to a student.

'Does it matter?' said Nyssa, descending the stairs.

The Doctor looked at her, surprised his deductions
were being so calmly dismissed. 'This is a very important
staircase. It connects the kitchen to the main hall.'

'Perhaps there's another way.'

The Doctor sat down on the bottom step. 'There's
something wrong. I can feel it.'

And he was right. If he had looked up at that
moment, he would have caught a brief glimpse of a
shadow on the landing. Instead he turned to Nyssa and
said, 'You'd better let the others in.'

'Shouldn't we get back to the TARDIS?'

'Soon. But first I want to consider this wall for a
little while.'

At the front door, Mace, realising there wasn't
anyone at home, had rediscovered his courage. Banging
on the door, he demanded to know where the Doctor
had got to and how much longer he would be. But such
was his manner and attitude neither Adric nor Tegan
felt inclined to find out for him.

But the swaggering rapidly ceased as the bolts were
heard being drawn back. The colour drained from
Mace's face. He almost seemed to shrink in stature. It

was far more than a change of mood, it was much more a complete metamorphosis. Tegan was stunned by his reaction.

As the door creaked open, Mace doffed his cap and gave a low, humble bow. This he held for a full fifteen seconds as he mentally went through his complete repertoire of totally cowed apologetic expressions. Selecting what he considered to be his most suitable, he straightened up and saw Nyssa smiling in the doorway.

'How did you get in?' said Tegan brightly.

'We found an open window.'

Mace's face collapsed into fresh grimaces of horror.

'You broke in?!' he spluttered.

'It's perfectly safe. There isn't anyone here. Come and look.'

With much coaxing and physical pushing from Adric and Tegan, Mace eventually followed Nyssa into the main hall.

'Where's the Doctor?' said Adric.

Nyssa led them across to the landing door. 'He's downstairs. He's found a wall that seems to fascinate him.'

'Any sign of survivors?'

Nyssa shook her head.

'Survivors?' Mace croaked. 'What is this talk of survivors?'

'The Doctor will explain,' said Nyssa, as she stepped out onto the landing. But she was mistaken. He had gone–disappeared. Anxiously, Nyssa looked around and then ran down the stairs calling for the Doctor.

'Where did you leave him?' said Tegan.

'Here on the bottom step. Staring at that wall.'

Tegan descended the stairs. 'Well, he can't be far.'

In turn their voices sang out, calling for him. Even Mace joined in. But as they continued to call, their voices grew more edgy, more concerned. At last too distraught to go on, Nyssa said distractedly, 'I shouldn't have left him alone.'

'And why not?' said the Doctor, as he appeared to pop out of a solid wall.

Concern instantly turned to amazement.

'That isn't possible,' said Tegan. 'No one can walk through a solid brick wall.'

'Quite right. So I used the door.'

Tegan was beginning to get annoyed. 'But there isn't a door. Your head is protruding from a solid brick wall!'

'The door's there. Only you can't see it.'

Nyssa approached the wall and ran her hands over it. 'It's an energy barrier.'

'Right.' The Doctor held up his sonic screwdriver. 'And I was able to part it with a sonic key.'

'Why can't we see through it?' said Adric.

'Camouflage. As you pass through it, it opens around you.'

Mace, who had been listening and watching said, 'Tell me this wall is a trick, an illusion. As a man of the theatre I am familiar with such things. But such a trick I've never seen before!'

'It's certainly here to deceive,' said the Doctor, hoping he wouldn't want details of how it worked.

'Incredible!' Mace felt the wall and then inserted his hand into the open part of the barrier. He turned to the Doctor, and beamed. 'With a trick like this, you could make a fortune around the fairs.'

'You could indeed,' the Doctor smiled. 'Come on,' he added, 'we must find the survivors.' And he disappeared again.

Mace patted the wall before passing through the invisible opening. 'I must learn how it's done,' he muttered.

As the companions followed the actor through the wall, the shadow of an enormous man wrapped in a cloak fell across the landing. Slowly the shadow spread across the floor, until its owner reached the top of the staircase. It was the android, beautiful and deadly, who had killed Sir John and his two children. He paused for a moment, then clipped on a mask and raised the hood of his cloak. Slowly he descended the stairs.

*

Cautiously, the Doctor and his party made their way along the passage, checking doors as they went, but with little success. They were all locked.

'What's that smell?' said Adric.

'Soliton gas.'

'I thought I recognised it,' said Nyssa.

Tegan coughed. 'Who'd want this sort of atmosphere? It's stifling.'

'Someone who needs it to breathe properly,' said the Doctor, trying the last door in the passage. The handle gave. 'This could be it.'

Carefully he inched the door open and purple light spilled into the passageway. The Doctor peered round the door and down into a cellar. No one was there. Slowly he allowed the door to swing open to its widest point. Cautiously he entered, and descended the steps.

Tegan followed. 'It's spooky,' she said.

In the purple gloom, hundreds of tiny cages could be seen stacked along one of the walls. At the far end of the cellar was an enormous rack containing dozens of bottles of wine. The others followed and started to explore the cellar.

'Doctor,' called Nyssa. She was standing in front of a green cylinder that was silently pulsating. 'It's the Soliton gas machine.'

With hand on pistol, Mace edged his way towards the wine rack. 'How is this place lit?'

'Vintaric crystals,' said the Doctor, joining Nyssa by the gas machine. 'It's quite a common form of lighting.'

'Really,' the actor grunted, unconvinced. The sight of so much wine was proving too difficult to resist. A bottle or two would help pull everything back into a more realistic perspective, he thought. With loving care, Mace withdrew a bottle from the rack. 'Nectar,' he whispered joyously.

Adric watched him. 'What does that stuff taste like?'

'Ambrosia!'

Adric thought for a moment. 'And what does that taste like?'

Mace scowled. Foolish boy, he thought.

While the Doctor and Nyssa continued their inspection of the Soliton machine, Tegan wandered about the cellar. As she drew near to the tiny cages, she heard squeaking. 'Doctor,' she said. 'These cages are full of rats.'

'Don't touch anything,' said the Doctor as he walked over to look.

Tegan screwed up her face in disgust. 'You must be joking. I feel itchy just looking at them.'

Silently and unnoticed, the android descended the stairs, wearing the mask of a grotesque death's-head. Draped in his heavy black cloak, all that it required was a scythe to complete the impersonation of Death, the Great Reaper.

Tegan moved away from the cages to the wine rack, where Richard Mace was struggling to remove the cork from a bottle. As she approached, he turned, proudly displaying his prize, his face covered with a large, silly grin. Tegan chuckled. 'Don't get too drunk.'

Mace didn't reply. Instead his expression turned to one of horror as he saw the black shape over Tegan's shoulder. Tegan turned to see what had scared him, while the actor started to scream.

'Don't!' the Doctor shouted, seeing Mace draw his pistols. But he was too late. The loud report of the discharged pistols echoed around the room.

The android, undamaged, lifted his hand as though to point. Blind with fear, Mace fled across the cellar and up the steps.

The android turned, his direction and range-finder locked onto the fleeing actor. Just as he fired, Adric leapt onto the android's back, causing the beam of energy to miss its target, but it hit Tegan instead, who immediately collapsed.

'Nyssa, run!' shouted the Doctor.

Confused and uncertain, she hesitated to move. 'What about you?'

'Just get out of here?'

Nyssa ran to the steps while a struggling Adric was effortlessly flicked from the android's back. The boy screamed as he rolled over in the air and struck the stone slabs of the floor. The android then turned towards the Doctor, who was sprinting across the cellar towards the Soliton machine. Again he raised his index finger and prepared to fire as the Doctor flung himself onto the gas unit and groped wildly for the controls.

The android paused as a loud hiss emitted from the machine.

'I don't know if you can understand me,' said the Doctor, climbing down from the Soliton unit, 'but I would like to point out how inflammable Soliton becomes when mixed freely with oxygen.'

Quickly he moved away from the machine and across the floor to Tegan. Lifting her arm, he felt her pulse: it was erratic. 'If you fire that beam of yours,' he continued, 'you'll turn this house into an inferno.'

The android lowered his hand and started to move towards the Doctor, forcing him to abandon Tegan and retreat to the cellar steps. Although his trick had worked, the android was still capable of crushing the Doctor in his steel fingers.

Reluctantly the Doctor backed up the stairs, but instead of following, the android side-stepped to the Soliton machine and readjusted the controls. It would take but thirty seconds before the Soliton level dropped sufficiently for the android to use his blaster.

Adric seemed to be recovering. 'I'll be back as soon as I can,' the Doctor shouted. But Adric didn't hear anything as he slipped back into oblivion.

Richard Mace charged into the main hall, wide-eyed with fear and panic. Thrusting his pistols into his waistband, he stumbled across the room, his only thought to get out of the house and as far away as possible.

'Wait,' shouted a breathless voice, but Mace didn't falter. 'Please wait.' A panting Nyssa tumbled into the room. 'We must help the Doctor.'

'Your Doctor is a dead man!' The actor fumbled with the handle of the door which led to the hallway. 'Did you not see who was in the cellar?' He threw the door open. 'It was Death, the Great Reaper!'

'That's what you're supposed to think.'

'Then what was it?' Mace was not keen to argue with a fool.

'An android, a mechanical man, a machine.'

'Perfectly correct,' said the Doctor, appearing at the landing door behind them.

Mace slowly turned, his terror renewed. 'You are supposed to be dead, sir,' he said, feeling for the reassuring shape of the crucifix under his shirt.

'Not this time.'

'Then your mind is addled! It was Death. You saw the effect my pistols had on him.'

'It takes more than a pair of flintlocks to damage an android.'

'Then there is no place in this house for me.' Mace disappeared into the hallway.

'Let him go, Doctor.'

'We need all the help we can get,' he said, crossing the room. 'Adric and Tegan are hurt.'

But Mace's only interest was getting the front door open.

'Death has them now,' he said over his shoulder. 'There is nothing I can do.' With the bolts released, the heavy door swung open and Mace stepped out into the sunlight. Nyssa and the Doctor followed.

'If it hadn't been for Adric, you would still be in that cellar.'

'I am grateful to the boy. But trying to rescue him would be nothing more than a futile gesture.'

Gravel spat from beneath the Doctor's boots as he angrily caught up with Mace and grabbed him by the neck of his leather jerkin, spinning him round. 'Now listen to me!'

'That isn't the way, Doctor,' said Nyssa.

He released the actor. 'I'm sorry,' he said a little awkwardly. 'I didn't mean to do that.'

Mace tugged at his jerkin, attempting to restore both its shape and his dignity. 'I realise how you feel about the boy,' he said at last. 'But I would rather be sealed up in a plague house than go back into that cellar.'

The Doctor ran his fingers nervously through his hair. 'Let me start again,' he said. 'The android, like the ornament around your neck, is not from this planet.'

Mace fingered the trinket. 'But I found it in the barn.'

'As we found this.' The Doctor removed one of the powerpacks from his pocket and held it up. 'That thing you're wearing isn't for adornment. It's part of what is called a control bracelet. A device used on prison planets to control difficult prisoners.'

Mace looked down on the ornament. 'How can this control anyone?'

The Doctor removed the ornament from Mace's neck and inserted the tongue of the powerpack into a small hole on the side of the design. Instantly the bracelet began to pulse. 'If that were on your wrist, you would have lost control of your mind by now.'

Mace laughed in a none-too-convincing way. 'A nonsense! The glow is a conjuring trick. You forget, sir, I am a man of the theatre. I am not impressed with such trickery, however clever it may be.'

'A trick, eh?' The Doctor disconnected the powerpack and thrust the now harmless ornament into

Mace's hand. Holding up the pack, he said, 'Well, this is a piece of conjuring you won't see done for many a year.'

The Doctor twisted the top of the cartridge, causing a massive bolt of electricity to zig-zag to the gravel driveway.

Mace leapt backwards, disturbed and uncertain what to believe. 'That's what happens when you discharge a powerpack,' said the Doctor discarding the spent pack.

The actor scratched the stubble on his chin.

'Do you still not believe the Doctor?' said Nyssa.

The problem was, Mace didn't trust or believe anyone. He had spent too many years as a confidence trickster himself, both on and off the stage, to believe anyone readily.

'How can that android, as you call it,' he said at last, 'come from another world? There aren't any. Any fool knows that.'

'There are many worlds in many galaxies...' He paused, noticing Mace's blank expression. The Doctor let out a loud, frustrated groan. 'Why are Earth people so parochial?' He abandoned any hope of being able to reason with Mace. 'Come on, Nyssa, let's go.'

'What about Adric and Tegan?'

'There isn't anything we can do until we have dealt with the android. And as Mr Mace won't help us, we must return to the TARDIS first.'

'For what? We haven't any weapons.'

'We'll try to modify the sonic booster.' His voice lacked confidence. 'If we connect it to the frequency accelerator we may get a high enough pitch to shatter the android's balance cones. We might even vibrate him to pieces.'

Nyssa's expression was fierce. She understood precisely what the Doctor hoped to achieve. She also knew the dangers and the fact that androids were almost indestructible without the correct weapons.

'You cannot afford to improvise against an armed machine,' she shouted angrily.

'What other choice do we have?'

The Doctor turned to Richard Mace, and as a parting gesture, pointed at the ornament around his neck. 'If you meet anyone wearing a bracelet like that, keep well away from them. Especially if it's pulsating.'

'I will.' Mace extended his hand and the Doctor shook it. 'Good luck, Doctor.'

The actor turned and set off across the lawn to the small gate set in the perimeter wall. Nyssa and the Doctor watched him for a moment.

'Will he be all right?' said Nyssa.

The Doctor nodded. 'Of that I have no doubt.'

Mace opened the gate and disappeared.

'If the sonic booster is to work,' said Nyssa, 'we'll have to get very close to the android.'

But before the Doctor could answer, the well-modulated plummy voice of Richard Mace boomed out from behind the wall. 'Doctor!' The old manor house picked up the urgency in the call and intensified it with a magnificent echo. 'Doctor! Come quickly!'

Chapter 5

Tegan's eyelids fluttered as though she were dreaming. Then suddenly she opened them as a sense of contentment and well-being flowed through her body. Gradually her eyes focused. Whether it was seeing the android, or because he pressed the button on a console nearby, she didn't know, but her contentment was instantly replaced by a searing pain in the area of her chest, where the stun beam had hit her.

Tegan struggled to sit up, but found that her wrists and ankles were secured to the large couch on which she was lying. Next to her was Adric, pinioned in a similar fashion.

'Are you all right?' he whispered.

Tegan nodded. 'Where are we?'

'I don't know.'

Although it caused her neck and back to hurt, Tegan momentarily lifted her head, craning to see as much as she could. The glimpse she got suggested they were in a massive computer room. Along one wall was a bank of monitors, most of which displayed indecipherable alien script.

She lifted her head again and looked in another direction. This time she saw a massive console with a myriad of tiny lights winking and flashing. Facing the console was a large, highback chair which completely hid its occupant. Next to the chair stood the android.

'Well?'

Tegan closed her eyes and concentrated on relaxing her neck muscles. 'We're not alone,' she said at last.

Adric struggled to look.

'Remain as you are,' a voice hissed.

'Who said that?' said Adric.

The voice didn't answer. Instead several strange beeping noises were heard and the purple light from the vintaric crystals was lowered.

Tegan and Adric looked at each other in amazement as a hologram image formed in the air above their heads. As the picture settled, they could see it was the Doctor.

'Who is this man?' the voice hissed.

Adric told him.

'And where does this Doctor come from?' There was a pause. 'I know he is not of this planet,' the voice continued more forcefully.

'That's rubbish,' said Adric.

The voice hissed and wheezed as though already bored with asking questions.

'The Doctor has a sonic device that he used to dismantle the energy barrier. He also has an understanding of the gas known as Soliton.'

'We don't know anything about that,' said Adric.

'You are wearing synthetic garments manufactured by technology unknown on this planet.' The hiss was beginning to verge on a roar. 'I am asking you for the last time: where are you from! Answer or you die!' Such was the tone of voice, Adric and Tegan were left in no doubt that the speaker wasn't bluffing. 'Tell me about your mode of transport,' he roared. 'Tell me now!'

They did. The sibilant voice became much more friendly and Adric and Tegan realised they had said too much.

'Where is the TARDIS?' said their interrogator.

'I don't know,' said Tegan a little too quickly. 'It's in the woods. Only the Doctor knows exactly where.'

'You are crew members?'

'That's right. Vital members!'

The air-borne hologram of the Doctor dissolved into a moving image of him running with Nyssa towards the small gate in the perimeter wall.

'Are you sure?' the voice panted. 'Your companions seem to be abandoning you.' The image showed them passing through the perimeter gate. 'Perhaps you over-rate your importance.'

The hologram faded.

'Activate the poacher and his aides.' The android obeyed instantly, gliding to the control-bracelet panel. 'I want them to bring me the Doctor.'

Switches were pressed and half a mile away in the forest instructions were received. Immediately, two villagers and the local poacher abandoned their respective tasks and made their way to a prearranged spot.

'Soon the Doctor will be my prisoner,' the voice purred, 'and his time machine will be mine.'

Tegan and Adric looked at each other in despair.

Richard Mace stood with mouth wide open, staring at the enormous shape.

'What is it?' he said, sounding as though he wasn't too certain he wanted an answer.

'It's an escape pod,' said the Doctor, casually strolling up its ramp.

'Do you think it wise to enter, Doctor?' said Nyssa urgently.

'Whatever was in this thing is now safely ensconced in the manor house.'

Mace looked up at the pod. It was huge, conical in form, and a beautiful shade of gun-metal blue. On its underbelly were savage black scars acquired during its rapid descent through the Earth's atmosphere. It had half buried itself on impact, throwing up tons of soil and vegetation.

Nyssa joined the Doctor on the ramp.

'Are you coming?' she said to Mace. The actor pointed to himself as though he was being selected from a crowd and was uncertain the invitation was directed towards him or someone standing nearby. 'Come on!' shouted Nyssa as she followed the Doctor into the pod.

Richard Mace gazed at the conical shape. He didn't want to go inside the curious structure, but neither did he want to wait in the forest, alone. Gingerly he mounted the ramp.

Inside the pod, the Doctor wandered around. 'The place has been stripped,' he said. 'And I bet the hardware's up at the house.'

Richard Mace stood in the hatchway and nervously peered inside.

'It's quite safe,' said the Doctor.

Cautiously Mace entered. 'You said it was an escape pod?'

'That's right. A sort of lifeboat. Only it comes from a ship that flies.'

Mace didn't believe a word.

'This is all that is left of the craft that brought the android to Earth.'

The actor smiled benignly, as though in the company of harmless fools and imbeciles.

'The lights you saw in the sky a few weeks ago', the Doctor said examining an insignia on an internal hatchway, 'were caused by the main part of the ship burning up in the atmosphere.'

'It's true,' said Nyssa.

'And how do you know these things?' asked Mace, his scepticism in no way concealed.

The Doctor smiled. 'That would be difficult to explain. But at least we're friendly.' He tapped the insignia on the hatch. 'Which is more than can be said for the owners of this ship.'

'Who are they?'

The Doctor turned from the hatchway. 'The insignia identifies them as Terileptils. A very clever race of warrior.'

'Warriors?' replied the actor dourly.

'Don't worry, they haven't come here to fight.'

If Mace believed the Doctor, it didn't reassure him, as his face remained drawn and tense.

'How many Terileptils could this pod carry?' said Nyssa, fiddling with the mechanism which operated the main door.

'That doesn't concern me at the moment. It's the number of androids there are. The Terileptils build those things too well.'

Silently the main door of the pod slid to.

'Are you sure the sonic booster can deal with them?'

The Doctor continued his tour of inspection.

'It has to. Their androids are programmed to protect. And the only way round them is to destroy them before they destroy you.'

This news didn't help to relax Mace's grey countenance either.

'Then we'd better hurry up with the booster.' Nyssa tapped the door-opening mechanism and watched the door slide open.

'A refresher course in android design would help,' added the Doctor.

'Android design?' Mace was flabbergasted. 'And how could you possibly get that?'

The Doctor paused in front of the actor and placed his hands together as though he were about to pray. 'Well,' he said, 'I too, have a ship of sorts.' The Doctor allowed his hands to drop to his sides. 'It isn't the most reliable of machines, but its aged memory-banks might contain something useful.'

'A ship,' said Mace doubtfully. 'Like this one?'

'Oh, no. Much more sophisticated,' Nyssa chipped in.

'And you are about to go there now?' Mace's delivery of this sentence was slow and measured; crisply enunciating each word to avoid any chance of misunderstanding.

'That's right.'

Then after a long moment, the actor said, 'May I come with you?'

'Are you beginning to believe me?' said the Doctor.

The actor indicated his surroundings. 'It seems I have little choice.'

As they emerged from the pod, Richard Mace questioned the Doctor closely concerning the secrets of how the sliding door worked. In his own mind the actor had already conceived a drama that not only featured such a door but also a wall that could be walked through. People would come from far and wide. He would be rich and famous.

But Mace's fantasy was interrupted by an urgent call from Nyssa. A hundred yards away stood three men, two of whom were armed with farm implements—a pitchfork and an axe—the other with a longbow.

The Doctor and Mace stopped at the foot of the ramp.

'Do you know who they are?' said the Doctor.

'They're from the local village.' Mace drew his pistols as the three men fanned out into an arc. 'The one with the bow is the poacher.'

'You can put those away.'

Mace frowned at the Doctor.

'Look at their wrists. They're wearing control bracelets.'

Mace cocked his pistols. 'In my experience, most men are cowards, sir. The poacher and his friends are no exception. They will run.'

The poacher fitted an arrow to his bow.

'The bracelets over-ride fear,' said the Doctor. 'The only way you will stop them, is to kill them. So back into the pod. They're only interested in me.'

'Let me kill them.'

The Doctor shook his head. 'At the moment there are only three. Fire those things and we could have a dozen to contend with.'

Mace opened his mouth to protest.

'Save your breath,' said the Doctor. 'Into the pod. And take Nyssa with you.'

Mace and Nyssa backed up the ramp, leaving the Doctor to face the poacher and his companions alone.

'Are you the Doctor?' the poacher asked him.

'I am indeed. How do you do?'

'You must come with us.'

'I think not.'

With Mace and Nyssa safely inside, the Doctor felt it was time for him to edge his way towards the hatch.

Although he talked constantly, bombarding their controlled minds with endless questions, they remained undaunted. The poacher raised the bow to the firing position, his powerful arm drawing back the bow string. The Doctor continued to chatter away, his

61

eye firmly fixed on the tempered steel arrowhead. He was now within a few feet of the hatch.

'Stop! Or I fire!'

'All right. I'll come with you.' The Doctor moved a step or two down the ramp. The poacher momentarily relaxed, allowing his bow to dip. Having anticipated this lapse of concentration, the Doctor turned, flung himself up the ramp and dived through the hatch. As he flew in, Nyssa hit the door-closing mechanism. The hatch started to slide to, but not before the poacher's arrow was able to find its mark in the padded bulkhead, only a few inches from the Doctor's head.

With the hatch tightly shut, it was difficult to tell which of the trio was shaking most.

'Are you all right?' said Nyssa.

The Doctor nodded as he climbed to his feet. As he did so, the pod started to echo with the sound of metal against metal.

'What's that?' demanded Mace.

'Our friendly neighbourhood axeman trying to break in.'

'He'll never cut through that hatch,' said Nyssa with relief.

'You're right.' The Doctor moved quickly to the far end of the pod. 'But he might get lucky and hit the opening mechanism on the outside.'

Mace again drew his pistols.

'Forget those. We can get out through the back door.'

The Doctor prodded the hatchway he had examined earlier. 'Emergency escape hatch. Crouch down.'

Such was the urgency in his voice, they obeyed without question.

Nyssa and Mace watched as the Doctor started to fiddle with the insignia on the hatch. First he pressed it, then carefully felt round its edges, searching for the release mechanism he knew must be there–somewhere.

'Can I help?' said Nyssa.

'Just stay where you are.'

The sound of the axe striking the main hatch grew more frantic as he tugged at the insignia. Suddenly the insignia gave with a jerk and twisted on its pivot, revealing a small hole. The Doctor inserted his finger and pressed. Nothing happened. He tried again. Nothing. 'I need a lever,' he called. 'I can't shift the release mechanism.'

Nyssa scuttled across the pod floor, extracted the poacher's arrow from the bulkhead and handed it to the Doctor.

'Excellent,' he said, inserting it into the hole and pressing it hard. There was a loud click and a small porthole opened, revealing the release handle. 'Are you ready?'

Nyssa crouched down by Mace.

The Doctor discarded the arrow, grasped the release handle and wrenched it down.

Suddenly the pod was filled with the piercing sound of a klaxon as a warning light built into the hatch started to pulsate. The Doctor quickly joined Mace and Nyssa, crouching down alongside them.

'What is this?' said Mace pointing at the emergency hatch.

'Just keep your head down.'

As the Doctor spoke, the explosive bolts were detonated, hurling the emergency hatch clear of the pod.

'Let's go!' The Doctor leapt to his feet and ran to the opening. 'Quickly!'

His companions needed no encouragement. Nyssa and Mace shot past the Doctor, out through the escape exit, into the sunshine and the forest.

The heavy wooden door slammed shut. Adric and Tegan stood in the middle of the cold dank room and dejectedly stared about it. Apart from a split palliasse and a wooden stool, the room was empty.

Adric crossed to the tiny window set high in the wall, and gazed at its heavy bars. 'Well, we won't get through those. Not without a cutting device.' He then walked around the walls tapping them, but their solidness absorbed the sound. Suddenly his frustration welled up and he hit the wall with the flat of his hand. 'I'm a fool!' he shouted. 'I should never have mentioned the TARDIS.'

'Don't let it get you down.' Tegan lowered herself onto the stool. 'If you hadn't told him, I would. I don't think he was kidding about torturing us.'

'We've got to get out of here and warn the Doctor.'

Tegan closed her eyes. She felt exhausted, a hundred years old. Her chest was still sore from where the stun ray had hit her. But most of all, she was afraid, more scared than she had ever been before. Her own mortality seemed to be staring her in the face. For the first time in her life she felt she might die.

Chapter 6

The poacher leapt from the ramp of the pod as the Doctor and friends disappeared into the forest. Flicking a switch on his control bracelet, he spoke into a tiny, concealed microphone.

'Have found the Doctor,' he said. 'At your craft. But has escaped. I am about to track him.'

'Wait!' The sibilant voice of the Terileptil Leader was heard. 'Follow but do not capture. Report when he reaches his own craft.'

The Doctor's party jogged on, but the portly Mace was suffering badly.

'I'm dead,' he shouted, coming to a sudden halt. 'My frame was never designed for rapid acceleration.'

Anxiously the Doctor glanced over his shoulder. 'You can't rest yet.'

But Mace wasn't listening. He staggered over to the stump of a tree and collapsed. Limply he pointed in the direction from where they had just come. 'They're not following,' he said, 'we're quite safe.' Suddenly he closed his eyes and allowed his head to topple forward onto his chest.

'Are you all right?' said Nyssa,

'No, madam,' he groaned. 'I am about to die.'

'You haven't got time,' said the Doctor.

Mace looked up at the Time Lord. 'You are a cruel man, sir. I cannot go on. I cannot move from this spot unless supported by a horse.' He mopped his brow with a filthy square of material. The thought of transport had cheered him considerably. 'The miller has one,' he continued. 'You could steal it.'

The Doctor's face suddenly lit up. 'Of course! The miller! Why didn't I think of him?'

'Doctor!' Nyssa glowered. 'You can't steal the poor man's horse.'

'Of course not! It's the man not the horse I'm interested in.'

Mace suddenly sat upright, a mean look on his face.

'The miller comes and goes at the house when he likes. Maybe he will help us—at least tell us what's going on up there,' the Doctor continued.

Nyssa frowned. 'Is that really such a good idea?'

'It's better we do.'

'It's better we leave the area, sir!' Mace chipped in.

The Doctor ignored the remark. 'Look, Nyssa, go back to the TARDIS and start work on the booster.'

'Alone?'

'You're more than capable.'

She was doubtful.

'I may not be able to find the miller. And we can't afford to waste time,' the Doctor insisted.

Reluctantly she agreed, but she wasn't very happy about it.

'I'll be back as soon as I can.'

'Even sooner if at all possible,' said Nyssa embracing the Doctor. 'Good luck.'

Mace and the Doctor watched in silence as Nyssa followed the pathway back to the TARDIS. Once she was out of sight, the Doctor turned to the actor and said with great urgency in his voice, 'Which way to the mill?'

But Mace was sulking. 'I cannot move, sir. My body has ceased to function.'

'Just direct me then. You can wait here for the poacher and his friends.'

Richard Mace looked down at the pistols he was carrying, then at the forest all around.

'You can't fight all of them,' said the Doctor. 'Kill the three who are following us and others will come to avenge their deaths.'

Uneasy, Mace rose from the stump. 'I'll show you,' he said, straightening his stiff back. 'But you have a mean way of exposing a man's cowardice.' With as much dignity as he could muster, Mace strode off into the undergrowth. The Doctor smiled, pleased the actor had decided to help.

Watching from high up in a nearby oak tree was a villager. Like those who had attacked them in the smoke, he was not wearing a control bracelet but a rough sacking mask over the lower part of his face.

As soon as the Doctor and friends were out of sight, he shinned down the tree and trotted back to his village to report their movements.

Tegan and Adric had inspected every inch of the room that was their prison cell.

'It's no use,' said Adric. 'We'll never get out of here.'

Tegan sat on the stool, fearing that he was right. The old house was too well built, its doors too solid. She allowed her eyes to wander around the room once again. Only this time they settled on the lintel of the door frame.

'Wait a minute,' she said, jumping up and dragging the stool across to the door. 'Look up here.'

Adric looked, but couldn't see anything to get excited about.

'There a fanlight above the door.' Tegan climbed onto the stool and examined the boards that were covering it.

'What's a fanlight?'

'A sort of window. If I can shift these boards, we might be able to get out.'

Tegan inserted her finger between the ill-fitting slats and started to pull. The nail securing the bottom of the board creaked and groaned as she lifted it. Tegan peered through the gap into the passageway outside. It was empty. She could also see that the glass in the fanlight was broken.

Tegan pulled again and felt the board give a bit more. 'Quickly,' she said, 'hold onto me.'

Adric wrapped his arms around Tegan's legs and braced himself against her with his shoulder. Given the extra support she was able to apply more leverage, but the board she wanted to move continued to resist.

'So near and yet so far,' she said, straining with all her might.

'Let me try. I'm stronger.'

'But not as determined.' Suddenly the bottom of the slat came away.

'Well done!'

With the top end of the board still attached to the fanlight frame, Tegan raised the plank back against its fixing, and cautiously peered out. Advancing along the passageway was the android, carrying a large wooden crate.

Tegan quickly withdrew her head.

'What is it?' said Adric in a low voice.

'The android.'

Silently they waited, listening to the rasp of steel on stone as the machine walked by. On hearing the cellar door slam, Tegan instantly set about freeing the remaining slats. She worked quickly and with determination although her arms and hands were sore and shaky with the unaccustomed effort.

With the last of the boards removed, she paused for a moment. 'I'm so unfit,' she muttered.

'Do you want me to go first?'

'Certainly not!'

And with more agility than Adric had expected, she pulled herself up, clambered through the fanlight and silently dropped to the floor in the passageway. She then moved quickly and quietly to the cellar door and listened. All was quiet but for the grunting and groaning of Adric as he half dropped, half fell to the floor. If Tegan hadn't been so scared, she would have been amused by the crumpled heap she saw.

'Come on,' she whispered, helping him to his feet. 'Let's get out of here.'

The Doctor and Mace crossed the clearing and peered into the rickety stable alongside the mill. The dull boom of a fast-running stream could be heard tumbling over the sluice, its power untapped, the water wheel stationary.

Silently they entered the stable. At one end was a harness room, its rickety clapboard door gently swinging on its hinges. Above them the well-stocked loft bulged with hay and straw. In the middle of the stable the miller's horse, hitched to a loaded wagon, patiently waited.

'Ah!' said Mace delightedly, 'the object of my desire.' Lovingly he patted and stroked the animal, then gently, reassuringly, blew into its nostrils.

'Hallo,' shouted the Doctor.

The sudden noise startled the horse, who snorted loudly. This was echoed by a donkey lurking in a stall at the back of the stable.

'Thievery,' said a disgruntled Mace, 'is a matter of stealth not hearty greeting, sir.'

'I'm here to see the miller, not to help you steal.'

'You are without pity, sir.'

The Doctor made his way along the side of the wagon towards the back of the building. As he did so he heard the plaintive squeaking of rats. At first he didn't pay much attention, but then realised it was coming from under the tarpaulin covering the load on the wagon.

The Doctor lifted the corner of the stiff, heavy cover expecting several bewildered rats to scurry out, but instead found that the wagon was loaded with cages full of the creatures.

Quickly, the Doctor re-covered the cages as the miller emerged from the harness room, whip in hand.

'Ah, good day,' said the Doctor cheerfully. 'Are you by any chance…' But the question remained uncompleted as the miller pushed by him and climbed up onto the box of his wagon. Undeterred the Doctor continued: 'I'll only keep you a moment.'

Richard Mace, who, on hearing the Doctor speak, had concealed himself behind the horse, now appeared, pistol in hand, and pointed it at the miller. 'You heard the gentleman,' he said in his best highwayman's voice. 'He only wants a word.'

Still the miller didn't respond. As he leant forward to pick up the reins, the Doctor saw he was wearing a control bracelet.

'Walk on!' shouted the miller, as he flicked the reins.

Mace cocked his pistol.

'Let him go,' said the Doctor.

Puzzled, Mace stepped to one side as the wagon lurched forward and rattled out of the stable. 'Why did you let him go?'

'He was wearing a bracelet,' said the Doctor.

'Him too.' Mace ran a hand over his stubbly jowls and looked worried. 'What is going on, Doctor?' he asked in concern.

'I wish I knew.'

*

Adric and Tegan burst into the main hall of the manor house, ran across the room and out into the hall. Out of breath, Adric fell on the bolts securing the front door and attempted to release them.

'Please hurry,' said Tegan nervously.

'I am.' Adric struggled with the bolts. 'But I can't shift them. It's as though they've been sealed.'

Tegan also tried but with equal lack of success. 'It will have to be the window.'

They ran back into the main hall and Adric scrambled up onto the sill and started to work on the window catches.

'How are they?'

'Stiff.' Suddenly the latch gave and the window was open. 'Quickly,' he said, extending an arm towards Tegan.

As she reached for Adric's hand, the landing door was pushed open by the android.

'Jump!' shouted Tegan.

But Adric hesitated. 'What about you?'

'Get out of here!' she screamed. 'Save yourself!' Adric still hesitated. In desperation Tegan threw herself against his legs, causing him to topple through the window. At the same moment, the android fired. The wall close to Tegan's head exploded, the shock waves throwing her to the floor.

'Run, Adric!' Tegan spluttered, a sudden inhalation of flying stone-dust causing her to choke.

Tegan looked up at the massive shape that was making its way towards her. Cautiously she got to her feet. Unable to think of anything more positive, she raised her hands and said in a dry, unnatural voice, 'I hope you realise I've surrendered.' She tried to sound flippant, but her voice lacked conviction.

The stable appeared empty but for Richard Mace and the donkey.

'Are you capable of carrying a tired thespian?' he muttered, staring into the animal's mournful eyes.

The Doctor emerged from the harness room and closed the door. 'Who were you talking to?'

Mace patted the donkey and smiled awkwardly. 'No one. I merely enquired after the donkey's health.'

The Doctor eyed the beast, realising what the actor was about. 'You're too heavy. He would never be able to carry you.'

Mace snorted. The donkey joined in in sympathy.

'Let's get back to the TARDIS and help Nyssa.'

'Not without the donkey,' he said firmly.

But their argument was curtailed as a dozen men suddenly poured into the stable and overpowered them. Kicking and struggling, both men were forced to their knees and Mace disarmed.

'We seem to have upset them,' grunted the Doctor as his arms were pulled back behind him.

76

A tall, thickly bearded man dressed in a shepherd's smock, detached himself from the main group of villagers. 'These people are plague-carriers,' he shouted.

'You jest, sir,' said Mace. 'We are free of the plague.'

'Quiet! The marks are apparent!'

The villagers shouted their agreement, although nothing could be seen. Their fear was justification enough for convicting the two outsiders.

'I can help you,' said the Doctor. 'We haven't got the plague.' He tried to reason with them, but they refused to listen.

'Execute them,' shouted a voice.

'Execute them indeed!' screamed the man in the smock.

Hands gripped the Doctor's head, and before it was pushed forward and his neck bared, he caught sight of a man moving across the stable carrying a large scythe.

'Oh no!' screamed Mace, as he realised the reason why a basket had been placed beneath his head.

The man with the scythe positioned himself carefully and raised his curved blade.

The villagers jostled each other excitedly.

'Now,' they shouted as one voice. The scythe hovered above the Doctor's bare neck.

'Wait!' a voice boomed from the stable door. The villagers turned. The man who had spoken out was the headman and with him was the poacher.

'They must die. They bring plague to the village,' the man in the smock said.

'These men are wanted criminals.' The Headman's voice was firm and authoritative. 'There is a reward.'

'What's the use of money if you're dead?' The scythe still hovered in the air. 'Kill them both!'

Rapidly the poacher fitted an arrow to his bow and raised it to the firing position.

'I am your Headman. You will listen to me!'

The villagers started to mutter among themselves, their voices indistinct, but their nodding heads and general demeanour seemed to indicate agreement to what had been said.

The scythe was lowered and the Doctor and Mace were helped to their feet. Both men were pale and a little unsteady after their experience.

'Thank you very much,' the Doctor said weakly. 'I can help you.'

But the Headman wasn't interested. Ignoring the Doctor he said, 'Lock them in the harness room.' He pointed to the shabby cupboard at the back of the stable. As he raised his arm, the Doctor noticed he was wearing a control bracelet.

Chapter 7

It wasn't until she arrived back at the TARDIS that Nyssa realised the size of the task she had agreed to undertake. It wasn't that the sonic booster was heavy. In fact, it was very light. But it was large, and so was the frequency enhancer she had to fit.

Trying to assemble the unit in the console room could cause problems, Nyssa decided, especially if the Doctor were to return and needed to move the TARDIS quickly, so she opted for her room as a more suitable place to work. Only after she had disconnected the booster from the base of the time rotor's pedestal and dragged it along the corridor did she realise she would also have to run a power cable to the room.

It took a little while before Nyssa was able to find a length of cable both long enough and of the correct rating to carry the heavy amperage the booster would require. Yet more valuable time was wasted as she fought to unwind its thick, python-like coils.

Nyssa groaned inwardly. Her arms ached, her fingers were sore and covered in small cuts. With more energy than was necessary, she thrust the cable into the power outlet at the base of the console's pedestal, and tightened the coupling clamp. But as she stood up, her anger turned to concern as she saw Adric on the scanner-screen running towards the TARDIS.

Quickly she operated the door-opening mechanism. A moment later a breathless Adric rushed in and collapsed in a heap.

Nyssa closed the doors and ran to help him.

'Adric! What's happened?'

But the boy didn't reply. He was very distressed.

Gently she said, 'Come and sit down.'

Adric didn't move, but continued to breathe heavily. At last he said, 'Where's the Doctor?', the words blurting out of his mouth.

'What's wrong?'

'I must talk to the Doctor.'

'He isn't here. He went to find the miller.'

'We've got to get back to the house. Tegan's still there.'

Nyssa placed her arm around his shoulder. 'What happened?'

'The android caught us escaping. And I had to leave her behind.'

'Was she hurt?'

'I don't know. We have to go back and find out.'

Nyssa was less certain. 'We should wait for the Doctor. We can't fight the android by ourselves,' she said.

Adric broke away from her comforting arm. 'Why isn't he here?' He slapped the console in anger. 'Why is he never around when you want him!'

With the door shut, the only illumination in the harness room came from the gaps between the shrunken boards of the walls. As though to tantalise them, the sun hurled shafts of white light through the gaps, creating a light/shade zebra-crossing effect on the floor.

The Doctor peered through a gap in the harness-room door at the villagers gathered in the stable, muttering. Although he was unable to hear what they were saying, the tone of their conversation was hostile.

With his back supported against a wall, Richard Mace sat illuminated in a shaft of light, wishing he were somewhere else.

'I have faced some of the most hostile audiences in the world,' he said mournfully. 'Earlier today I met Death in a cellar...' His mournfulness had now acquired a slightly dramatic tone. '...but I have never been so afraid as when I saw the man with the scythe.'

The Doctor wasn't listening, having heard the performance several times already. Instead, through his spyhole, he watched the Headman gesticulating wildly, the control bracelet on his wrist pulsating. 'Did you notice what the Headman is wearing?'

Mace looked up, annoyed at being interrupted in full flow. 'Should I care? He saved our lives.'

'For the Terileptils.'

'I thought you wanted to meet them.'

'Not as their prisoner.'

Mace clambered to his feet. 'I tell you, sir, I have reached the end.' This time the tone of his voice was without histrionics. 'I feel my mind slipping into a bottomless pit of despair and gloom.'

'Then you'd better snatch it back quickly,' the Doctor said, turning briskly from the door. 'The Headman's coming. I want to get the bracelet off.'

Mace's heart sank. 'That sounds like a dangerous plan, sir.'

'There's no alternative. Once he's free of it, we might be able to reason with him.'

The door of the harness room was thrown open and the Headman and the poacher entered, along with the sound of angry mutterings from the villagers in the stable. The poacher moved behind Mace.

'You are to be taken to the manor house,' said the Headman.

'Of course!' The Doctor was full of false enthusiasm. 'But first let me thank you for saving our lives.' The Headman didn't respond, although the Doctor extended his hand in friendship.

'To the manor with them!'

The poacher started to jostle the actor towards the door. Hoping Mace would back him, the Doctor grasped the Headman's hand. But instead of shaking it, he released the powerpack from the bracelet. The Headman screamed loudly, lashed out, then stumbled disorientatedly across the stable. By the time the Doctor had recovered from the attack, the harness-room door had been slammed and locked.

Meanwhile Richard Mace, prompted as much by a startled reflex response to the Doctor's sudden movements as by the rediscovery of his courage, had delivered a hard thrust of his elbow into the poacher's stomach. Whatever the stimulus, the effect had been startling: the man collapsed stunned.

Mace watched dejectedly as the Doctor disconnected the powerpack from the poacher's bracelet. 'That didn't get us very far,' he said.

'It was worth a try,' said the Doctor as he wandered back to his spyhole in the door.

'So what do we do now, sir?' He looked down at the body at his feet. 'Ransom the poacher? Exchange his life for our freedom?'

'I don't think they would be interested.'

'You are right, sir! The next time that door is opened, we are dead!'

The Doctor didn't need to answer. He knew what the actor said was true. The villagers were angry and scared. They needed but the smallest excuse to give vent to their frustration.

Through his spyhole the Doctor could see the man in the smock, playing on the villagers' fear.

'You must remember!' he shouted harshly at the Headman. 'What is it you want with this Doctor?'

'I don't know... I was working... Repairing a plough.' Frantically the Headman searched for a way to unlock his memories.

'Then what?' the man in the smock urged.

'I was heating the forge.' He paused. In his mind's eye he could see the white-hot hearth. 'I was pumping the bellows...' He paused again. 'Then I heard...' he said very slowly, '...a voice.'

The man in the smock fell on the statement. 'A voice?'

The Headman was distraught. '"Find the Doctor," it said. "Find the Doctor and bring him to me."' He was now shaking uncontrollably. 'Then I saw a picture inside my head.'

'A vision?' The villagers grew even more unsettled.

The Headman placed his hands over his face. 'It was horrible. I couldn't control my mind. I could only do what this voice said.'

'You were possessed!' screamed the man in the smock, turning to the other villagers. 'There is evil at work here. The plague-carriers are warlocks as well!'

The Doctor, who was still at his spyhole, had seen and heard everything. So had Mace.

'Our jailers sound decidedly against us,' the actor said, bending down to examine the poacher.

The Doctor began to move quickly around the room. 'There must be a way out of here.'

Mace pulled a dagger from the top of the poacher's boot. Holding it up he said, 'I could test the strength of this blade against the planking of the wall.'

At the manor house, two lights pulsed on the control-bracelet panel, indicating the disconnected powerpacks of the Headman and the poacher.

The Terileptil Leader watched. Under normal circumstances he would have taken delight in coping with the Doctor's interference. But there was still too much to do, and time was of the essence. The Doctor would have to be stopped before his activities became more than merely aggravating. He also needed the TARDIS.

The Leader turned to the android. 'Go,' he said. 'Fetch the Doctor and his friend.'

Without hesitation, the android glided out of the laboratory, across the cellar and past Tegan, who was seated at a rough, wooden table, a control bracelet fitted to her wrist. Carefully, with very precise movements, she packed small blue ampoules into reinforced carrying boxes.

Before climbing the cellar steps, the android wrapped his cloak around his shoulders and fitted his death's-head mask. Again he was every inch the Great Reaper.

When the android had gone, the Leader spoke into his communicator, informing his comrades, who were already at their town base, that his work was nearly complete and that he would be joining them as soon as it grew dark and was safe to travel. But it was the news that he had discovered the Doctor and his time machine that drew an enormous hiss of pleasure and satisfaction from his fellow Terileptils.

Adric sat on Tegan's bed and watched Nyssa attach the frequency enhancer to the sonic booster. Although outwardly he was much calmer, he was still concerned about Tegan.

With the enhancer in place, Nyssa used a magnetic clamp to secure it. The machine looked very clumsy and top heavy.

'It looks very vulnerable,' said Adric.

Nyssa nodded. 'It really needs an energy barrier to protect it.'

'Can't you fit one?'

'I don't have the components.' Nyssa looked worried. 'I wish the Doctor would hurry up. He knows far more about these things than I do.'

Adric slid from the bed and crossed to the door. 'Didn't you say he'd gone to the mill? I'll go and look for him.'

'No! If you miss each other we'd have to send out a search party for you.'

Adric paused at the door. 'I lack the skill to help you with the booster,' he said. 'I want to do something.'

Nyssa smiled weakly; she knew how he felt. 'Look,' she said, gently, 'the sooner the booster is finished, the sooner we can get back to the house for Tegan.'

Adric nodded. But it didn't help his feeling of helplessness.

'And cheer up,' she said. 'Being sad isn't going to help Tegan.'

Dust flew everywhere as bales of straw were thrown down from the loft in the stable. Eager hands grappled with them as they were dragged outside to build a bonfire. The man in the smock, his face red with excitement, urged the villagers on.

'Come on, lads! Quick as you can! Let's have them burnt before they can work any more of their magic!'

In the harness room, the two alleged warlocks worked away at the planking.

'I fear the man who built this wall knew his trade too well,' said Mace.

'We must keep trying.'

Mace worked at the timber with the knife. 'If only we possessed the skills of which we are accused. A small spell would work wonders.'

'Keep trying.' But the words were no sooner out of the Doctor's mouth than Mace was sent stumbling across the room, as the planking he was working on was punched inwards. Stunned, Mace watched in horror as other planks were splintered and wrenched from their place. The pounding continued until the hole was large enough to admit the android, cloak billowing, his death's-head almost seeming to glow.

Mace crouched in the corner where he had fallen.

'It's all right,' said the Doctor, helping the terrified actor to his feet. 'He isn't here to harm us.'

'How can you be so sure?'

'If he were, we would be dead already.'

Although unable to speak, the android made it very clear that they should follow him. Slowly Mace walked towards the hole.

There were raised voices in the stable. Someone shouted, 'Quickly! The warlocks are escaping.'

Rapidly the bolts were drawn and the harness-room door thrown open. Expecting to see the Doctor and Mace, the villagers were greeted instead by the android, his massive body filling the doorframe.

'Death!' screamed the man in the smock. 'The warlocks have summoned up Death.'

The villagers turned and fled from the stable, screaming, tripping, scrambling, falling over themselves in their panic.

Thankful to have escaped the bloodthirsty villagers, it was nevertheless with heavy hearts that the Doctor and Richard Mace followed the android out of the stable.

Chapter 8

The walk through the woods should have been enjoyable. The late afternoon sun was still pleasant and warm. Smoke from the purification fires hung in the trees, as though undecided where to go next. Birds sang, as a very slight breeze rustled their feathers. It was as though Nature had decided to show herself at her best, to convince those who had time to consider such things that she was capable of creating more than plague, fear and violent death. But the Doctor and Richard Mace were among those too preoccupied to appreciate the gesture.

They trudged on, supervised by the android, through undergrowth, along paths and across small clearings, until they finally came to the Terileptil's escape pod. Then on through the side gate, across the lawn and up the crunchy, gravel path. But they did not go to the front door. Instead they were directed around the west side of the house, then right again, to the tradesmen's entrance, where the miller's wagon was waiting.

The long corridor that led to the cellar was dark after the sunlit wood. It also smelt of Soliton gas. Their journey was almost over.

In the cellar Tegan continued to pack the last of the ampoules into a reinforced carrying case, the bracelet on her wrist pulsing in rhythm with her heart. She did not even look up, her concentration fixed solidly on her task, when the cellar door opened and Mace and the Doctor stumbled in.

'Tegan!' shouted the Doctor, relieved to see she was safe.

She turned towards him as he descended the stairs, her expression blank, as though her personality, her very essence, had been drained out of her.

'Yes?' she said.

The Doctor was almost alongside her. 'Concentrate,' he shouted. 'You can over-ride the effect of the bracelet. Concentrate hard!' He reached out and started to shake her. 'Get back to the TARDIS and tell Nyssa what's happened.'

Her empty face stared back.

'You must concentrate on what I'm saying.' Her eyelids started to flicker, but whether she had understood, the Doctor was not to find out, as the android gently but firmly pushed him on.

As they approached the far end of the cellar, the camouflaged energy barrier dissolved, revealing the Terileptil's laboratory beyond. Richard Mace stared at the hole, his desire to understand and exploit the illusion but a distant memory. How could so much happen in one day? he thought.

'You'd better prepare yourself for a shock,' the Doctor whispered.

Horrified, Mace turned to the Doctor.

'Now what?' he croaked.

'I don't think you'll have seen anything quite like a Terileptil before.'

The Doctor was right. The Terileptil Leader stood just over seven feet tall, with the immediate appearance of a massive bipedal reptile. His head was not unlike that of a Tyrannosaurus Rex, only smaller and with a shorter snout. But any thought of the head containing a dinosaur's peasize brain would have been dispelled by one glimpse of the lively, intelligent, magenta eyes. Instead of hair, the crown of the head was covered with tiny, flat orange fins, which continued down the back of his neck, where they grew thicker, swelling out where they met the finely scaled epidermis like a ruff. Although everything was totally alien about the Terileptil, there was a strange beauty about him. His lean, graceful features were arrogant and proud. Even to Richard Mace's tired, bewildered mind, the Terileptil carried himself with great authority and dignity, which made him appear overwhelming rather than terrifying.

'Are you all right?' whispered the Doctor. Mace nodded as the Terileptil strutted up to them. 'How do you do? I'm the Doctor,' he said affecting a totally false note of confidence. 'Are you in charge here?'

'You will remain silent,' hissed the Leader.

'Sorry. It's just that I'm rather concerned about a couple of friends I had to leave here,' the Doctor continued, trying to sound chatty. 'I've just seen Tegan, but I would like to know that the boy Adric is safe.'

'I have no interest in your friends.'

'That's unfortunate. Because our original purpose in coming here was to help you.'

'Help?' the Terileptil's voice was harsh and disbelieving. 'You would help a Terileptil?'

'To get back to his home planet, yes.'

The Leader let out a long, loud hissing roar. Simple reflex response to the sound propelled Mace one step backwards.

'You must think me a fool,' said the Leader.

'Not at all.'

'Look at me, Doctor.' The Terileptil lowered his own head as he pulled the Doctor towards him. 'Do you see this?'

Up until that moment the Leader had allowed no more than a three-quarter view of his face. He now

94

turned to reveal, on the left side, a large carbuncle-like growth and heavy scarring that covered his whole cheek.

'This disfigurement is not natural to my physiognomy,' said the Leader. 'There is only one place in the universe I could have received such scarring: the Tinclavic Mines of Raaga. And to be sentenced to Raaga is always to be sentenced for life.'

He released the Doctor and pushed him back.

'Ah,' said the Doctor awkwardly. 'I should have guessed. But Terileptian law was never my strong point.'

'But you understand now? I am a fugitive, Doctor. The last place I wish to go is home.' The Terileptil strutted away.

'I can see your point, but there are countless uninhabited planets where you could settle. You don't need to stay on Earth.'

'You imagine we would condemn ourselves to a primitive life without grace or beauty,' the Leader hissed.

'You're highly intelligent. You have your android, your skills. Your way of life wouldn't be primitive for long.'

The Leader snorted, as though in contempt.

'I can take you anywhere you want,' the Doctor continued. 'A billion light years from your home planet. You'd never be found.'

'No, Doctor.' The Terileptil's magenta eyes stared down at him. 'A barren rock in space without a ship is not an acceptable alternative. Especially when offered by someone who is my prisoner and their ship is for the taking.'

'You didn't look after your own ship very well. I gather its break-up made a very impressive spectacle.'

Slowly the Terileptil turned on the Doctor, the fins on the back of his neck gently rippling. The Doctor had said the wrong thing. Even if he hadn't known the significance of the fins, the way they moved now said it all. The Leader was very angry.

'It cost the lives of all but myself and three comrades.'

'There are only four of you?' Although the Doctor's tone was basically one of surprise, the hint of relief was too strong for the Leader to leave it unchallenged.

'It will please you to learn that we are now but three,' he snarled. 'But it is enough!'

'Against the millions who already live here?' The Doctor's response was now urgent. 'You'll never be able to establish yourself on this planet.'

The Leader's fins began to settle as he crossed to the control bracelet console. 'You are assuming we plan to co-exist.'

There was a nasty pause.

'Genocide?' the Doctor said slowly.

Never having heard the word before, Mace turned to the Doctor confused.

'The primitives on this planet are too aggressive and wilful,' the Leader bellowed before Mace could speak. 'We have little need for them, especially now we have your TARDIS.'

'That won't help you!' said the Doctor angrily. 'And you'll find their elimination far more difficult than you think.'

The Doctor found he was wagging his finger at the Leader like an angry schoolteacher might at a difficult class of children. He felt silly and even more frustrated because he had been reduced to such a ridiculous gesture.

Richard Mace was less inhibited. 'This thing is talking of mass murder!' he shouted.

The Doctor grabbed the actor's arm as he started to move towards the Terileptil. 'This is not the time to become heroic,' he warned.

'Heroic!' Mace bellowed. 'Do not humour me, sir!' he said, breaking away from the Doctor.

The Leader stared down at Mace. 'Is he a primitive?' His question was directed towards the Doctor which only added to the actor's annoyance.

'Primitive! Primitive!' he shouted. 'There is nothing primitive about me, sir!'

Such was the dignity the actor managed to get into such a banal statement, the Doctor almost wanted to cheer.

'So much pride', the Terileptil said contemptuously, 'in something so stupid!'

The Leader reached for his blaster. 'I should destroy you now.'

'Let me see you try!' Mace shouted as he rushed at him. But his gesture was in vain. Effortlessly he was flicked away with such force that he stumbled and fell on the floor in a crumpled heap.

'Fit the primitive with a bracelet,' the Leader said to his android. Instantly the order was obeyed.

'It won't all be as easy as that,' the Doctor said pointing to Mace. 'He is only one untrained man. What will you do when they send thousands of their soldiers against you?'

The Leader curled back his thick upper lip and exposed a row of beautifully even teeth.

'You are right, Doctor.' The Terileptil was, in fact, smiling. 'We cannot fight as warriors,' he said triumphantly, 'but I have already devised a plan that will make that unnecessary.'

'How?'

'You will find out, Doctor... before you die!'

*

Nyssa tentatively attached a magnetic drone to the booster. She wasn't happy. She had already exceeded her knowledge and was now working blind. This wouldn't have concerned her so much if the successful completion of her work hadn't been so urgent.

Adric entered carrying a carbon rod. 'Is this what you want?'

'Yes.'

Nyssa took it from him, flicked open the drone and inserted the rod.

'Is that it?'

'No,' said Nyssa. 'There are several fine adjustments to make...' She paused, looking somewhat dejected. 'To be honest, I'm not sure how to make them.'

'I knew it!' Adric crossed to the door. 'I'm going to find him,' he said and disappeared into the corridor.

'Please Adric!' Nyssa ran after him. 'What happens if you get lost?'

Adric didn't answer as he pushed open the console-room door, crossed to the scanner-screen control and operated it.

'You say you're concerned about Tegan,' said Nyssa as she followed him into the room. 'We can't help her without the Doctor's knowledge. It's dangerous to try and do anything without consulting him first.'

'So you keep saying. That's why I'm going to fetch him.'

Nyssa was beginning to get angry. 'No!'

Adric flicked a switch and watched as the image on the screen panned round. The woods, bathed in a yellow glow from the setting sun were deceptively quiet and beautiful.

'Have you not considered', said Adric as the image came to rest, 'that the Doctor might be in trouble.' He looked pointedly at Nyssa. 'He has been gone a long time.'

'He is quite capable of looking after himself.'

Adric operated the door-opening mechanism. 'That's the impression he always likes to give.'

Nyssa continued to argue, explaining her fears, appealing to his reason with as many arguments as she could muster. Even the reminder that the woods were full of hostile villagers didn't deter him. At last she relented and said, 'Where will you go?'

'To the mill.'

'Then you'll need this.'

She removed a torch from her tool box and checked to see that it was in working order.

'Take care,' she said, handing it to him.

Adric smiled awkwardly and left.

Nyssa closed the door and watched him on the scanner-screen, walking away from the TARDIS. The light was now beginning to fade rapidly, the glow of the setting sun finding it more and more difficult to penetrate the deep shadows.

Knowing Nyssa would be watching, Adric quickly turned and waved. As he turned to continue his journey, he found his way barred by two masked villagers. Quickly the boy spun round, but a third man was behind him, cutting off his retreat.

Nyssa watched, frantic, as he was led away. She opened the door and was about to run out into the woods, but realised there was little she could do, and her capture certainly wouldn't help anyone.

Reluctantly, she closed the door and walked dejectedly along the corridor, back into her room.

The sonic booster stood in the middle of the floor, wires hanging from it like tendrils from a plant.

Nyssa stood before the machine. Such was her state of mind it seemed to mock her, reminding her of her helplessness. She felt wretched, frustrated and alone.

Suddenly she turned on the sonic booster in a fit of wild anger. 'Stupid machine,' she shouted and started to kick it hard.

Lazily, the miller's horse looked up from munching a pile of hay as Mace and Tegan, controlled by the bracelets they were wearing, loaded down with reinforced ampoule-boxes, emerged from the manor house.

An early evening badger poked his head from a nearby bush and for a moment watched the strange procession, before setting off in search of supper.

Held firmly by the android, the Doctor, too, was part of the procession, only his journey was from the Terileptil's laboratory to the cellar.

The android halted near the Terileptil who was rummaging in a large box near the table where Tegan had been working. Slowly he rose clutching a pair of ancient handcuffs.

'Don't I qualify for a control bracelet?' said the Doctor.

'Your mind would over-ride the effect.'

'I wouldn't be too certain.'

The Leader's lip curled in a sort of smile as he snapped the handcuffs onto the Doctor's wrists.

'Cruder, but more effective, I think.'

The Doctor held up his hands and rattled the chain connecting the cuffs, as though testing their strength. 'Tell me,' he said, 'what happened to the occupants of this house?'

'A noble death. They were allowed to die fighting.'

The Terileptil raised a webbed hand and the android escorted the Doctor across the cellar towards the steps where he halted.

'Do you enjoy killing?' the Doctor shouted back over his shoulder.

The Leader hissed. 'We are at war, Doctor. And war is honourable. Even on this planet it is considered so.'

'I know...' The android prodded the Doctor indicating he ascend the steps. 'But by your own admission, these people are still primitive. What's your excuse?'

The android placed a steel hand on the Doctor's shoulder and squeezed, causing the Doctor to wince.

'Take him away!' commanded the Leader.

Far more roughly than was necessary, the Doctor was dragged up the steps and along the corridor to where Adric and Tegan had been held prisoner.

While the android opened the door, the Doctor saw Richard Mace enter the tradesmen's entrance at the far end of the corridor. Although the Doctor shouted, the actor didn't respond. A moment later he was thrust into the room and the door slammed shut and was locked behind him.

Despondently the Doctor looked around, the room now completely bare, the stool and palliasse having been removed after Tegan and Adric's escape. Even the fanlight had been sealed again, this time with heavy beams of timber.

The Doctor looked down at the handcuffs. Old-fashioned though they were, without some way of unlocking them they were as effective as any sophisticated device.

Quickly the Doctor searched in his pockets for his sonic screwdriver. Finding it proved easier than removing it from the tangled lining of his jacket. As he tugged and pulled, other objects trapped in the folds of the pocket—safety-pins, the powerpacks found in the barn, coins of uncertain denomination and origin—cascaded to the ground. The Doctor bent down and started to gather them together. 'I must get a proper survival kit together one day,' he muttered.

With the screwdriver free, he set about trying to release himself from the cuffs. Although the sonic device was more than capable of dealing with the crude works, manipulating the screwdriver was made difficult by the very short chain connecting the cuffs.

Several minutes passed as he continued to tussle, but he couldn't quite line up the sonic beam with the lock. His task was made more arduous and painful as the friction from the cuffs had started to skin his wrists.

'Oh, for a proper key,' he muttered, and sat back on his haunches to rest for a moment. At that moment he heard the sound of a key in the door.

Speedily, the Doctor picked up one of the powerpacks and the safety-pins, and was stuffing them back in his pocket as the door was pushed open.

'Stay where you are, Doctor,' the Leader hissed.

He froze as the Terileptil strutted into the room, stun gun in hand.

'You are a foolish man, Doctor,' the Leader said, his eyes falling on the screwdriver. 'Drop the sonic device.'

He obeyed, sending the silver shape slithering across the floor. As it came to rest, the Leader fired, and the sonic screwdriver exploded, bursting into flames.

The Doctor looked at the twisted strip of smouldering metal, unable to believe what he saw. 'I feel as though you've just killed an old friend.'

'And soon you will join it.'

As the Leader spoke, Tegan, carrying a large covered box entered the room and placed it on the floor near the Doctor. Behind her came Richard Mace carrying a pistol.

'It saddens me that you should die,' said the Terileptil, 'but if I allowed you to live you would be a greater menace than all the primitives on this planet.'

'I think you overestimate me,' said the Doctor, looking suspiciously at the box Tegan had brought into the room.

'But there would be the argument over the TARDIS.' The Leader nodded to Tegan who started to uncover the container. 'I said I would demonstrate how I am to rid the planet of its primitive inhabitants,' said the Leader, the sibilance of his voice becoming more pronounced as though he were excited or stimulated in some way.

Tegan dragged the cover from the box to reveal a cage full of black rats.

'The infection the rats now carry,' the Terileptil continued, pointing at the box, 'has been genetically re-engineered. Though heavily infected, they will outlive you all.'

The Doctor looked puzzled. 'But you'll need thousands of them.'

The Leader's lip curled in an ugly smile.

'We have thousands. They are awaiting release in a nearby city. Their infection will kill every living thing,' he said, almost proudly.

'I thought the local plague was already doing that.'

Slowly the Doctor began to edge towards the box.

'Our rats will ensure there are no survivors.'

'A final visitation,' the Doctor muttered.

'Precisely! We do not need the primitives. Now we have your TARDIS we will be able to travel to any part of the Universe and acquire androids.'

'Such carnage isn't necessary!' The Doctor was angry.

The fins on the Terileptil's neck rippled slightly.

'It's survival, Doctor,' he hissed. 'As these primitives kill lesser species to protect themselves, so I kill them.'

'That's hardly an argument!'

'It isn't supposed to be.' The Leader strutted to the door. 'It's a statement!' His voice was harsh. 'If you try to interfere with the cage, your friends' controlled minds contain but one thought...' he turned to face the

Doctor, his massive bulk framed in the doorway, '...and that is to kill you.'

The Doctor could only watch as the heavy door was slammed shut and locked.

Mace and Tegan continued to stare about them, their expressions blank.

Urgently the Doctor turned his attention to Tegan. 'I know you never listen to what I say...'

She blinked back at him.

'...but please put the cover back over the cage.'

Tegan remained perfectly still, the bracelet on her wrist pulsing all the while.

'You can do it.' The Doctor made a sudden move towards the box, but Mace instantly raised his pistol and cocked it.

The Doctor stopped dead in his tracks and raised his hands.

'Just concentrate, Tegan' he continued, his voice insistent. 'Just concentrate and you can over-ride the control... think hard.'

She didn't move, just continuing to blink. The whole rhythm of her body seemed to be keeping time with the pulsating bracelet.

'Cover the cage, Tegan!'

This time she did respond and bent down to the cage. The Doctor breathed a sigh of relief, but it was premature. Instead of covering it, she started to unfasten its door.

'No! Don't open it!'

She continued to fiddle with the catch.

'If you do, it's the end for us all!'

But Tegan didn't respond.

Suddenly the Doctor remembered the powerpack he was still holding. Gingerly he fingered it, uncertain whether its charge would be strong enough. He looked at Mace and then at his pistol. He could not let Tegan open the cage. He had to risk it, knowing that if he failed the actor would kill him.

Tentatively, he angled the powerpack towards the barrel of Mace's pistol and twisted the top. A bolt of electricity shot from the pack, but instead of zig-zagging to earth, as it had done before, it leapt towards the barrel of the gun.

The actor let out a loud scream, dropped the pistol and staggered around for a moment before collapsing. Tegan abandoned her work on the catch and made a lunge for the pistol, but the Doctor's foot got to it first and set it spinning across the floor out of reach.

Tegan jumped to her feet and adopted an aggressive pose.

'We haven't got time to fight,' the Doctor said urgently.

But Tegan didn't agree. Her foot shot forward forcing the Doctor to jump backwards to avoid the blow. He knew that although Tegan was physically small she was strong. And as his hands were still cuffed, the chances of her delivering a knock-out blow were greatly increased.

Tegan lashed out again, but the Doctor was able to sidestep the attack. She kicked again, this time overbalancing. The Doctor quickly grabbed her arm, swung her round and pinned her against the wall with his shoulder. Tegan continued to struggle, trying to punch and bite. But trapped as she was, the Doctor was able to use his additional weight and strength to restrain her while he disconnected her bracelet.

Instantly Tegan stopped fighting and slowly slithered down the wall.

The Doctor moved quickly to the cage of rats and checked that it was still fastened. He then crossed to where Richard Mace was lying stunned and released the powerpack from his bracelet. As soon as he had freed it, Mace sat bolt upright.

'What happened?' he demanded in an almost perky voice.

Suddenly the Doctor felt very tired. 'Just relax for a moment,' he said sitting on the floor next to the actor. 'You'll be all right.'

Mace looked at the Doctor. 'And how do you know?'

The Time Lord sighed. 'Because I'm the Doctor...'

On the other side of the room Tegan started to groan. She was beginning to recover.

With a sigh of relief, the Doctor realised that he didn't have to worry about his two fellow prisoners any more. They would both be fine.

He cast his eyes over the heavy door of the room. Getting through it would be the next problem.

Chapter 9

Awkwardly, the Leader, now wearing a long black cloak, lumbered along the corridor and out through the tradesmen's entrance into the steel-blue light of the early evening. Deprived of Soliton gas, the Terileptil wheezed and gasped as he made his way to the waiting wagon. Slowly he climbed onto its box, aided by the android.

Once settled, he wrapped the heavy cloak around his legs and pulled the hood over his head to hide his reptilian features.

'Go,' the Leader rasped to the android. 'Search for the TARDIS. When you find it, pilot it to the base in the city.'

Silently the massive android turned, fitted his death's-head mask and strode off towards the forest, while the miller loaded the last of the ampoule boxes on to the wagon.

'Cover them quickly.'

The miller obeyed, pulling the heavy tarpaulin in place.

'Now return to the laboratory. You have my instructions.'

As the miller returned to the house, the Terileptil picked up the reins, flicked them and the wagon moved off along the driveway.

Having locked and bolted the door, the miller then made his way along the dark corridor, through the cellar to the laboratory, where he operated the energy barrier switch and sealed himself in. His instructions were to wait, to guard the labratory if necessary with his life, an order his controlled mind would not hesitate to obey.

The miller then crossed to the corner where his provisions were stored, picked up a flintlock pistol and started to prime it.

'How do you feel?' said the Doctor.

'Groggy, sore and bad-tempered,' moaned Tegan.

'Almost your old self!'

Tegan scowled at the Doctor. 'That's not funny,' she said. 'And why is he in such good spirits?'

Richard Mace was striding up and down the room as though he had just awakened from twelve hours' deep restful sleep. He turned and grinned his broadest cavalier grin and said, in his best, richest, plummiest voice, 'Madam! I am a man of iron.'

Seated next to Tegan on the floor, the Doctor looked up at the actor with tired eyes. 'More likely the electric charge I gave him from the powerpack. It's over-ridden the side effects of the bracelet.'

'Can't you do the same for me?'

'Too dangerous.' The Doctor scrambled to his feet. 'Exercise is much safer and just as effective.'

Tegan grasped the Doctor's offered hand and stood up. She felt dreadful, as though suffering from a bad dose of flu. 'Now what?' she groaned.

He rattled the chain connecting his handcuffs. 'First, I must lose these.'

'Never fear!' said Mace at his most theatrical. 'I am at hand.'

The Doctor and Tegan looked at each other, wondering what he meant.

'What can you do?' she said.

'Do you have some wire?' purred Mace. Suddenly he was in his element. He could do something positive. And when centre stage, he revelled in the enjoyment of his performance.

'Will this do?' said the Doctor, producing a safety-pin.

'Perfect!'

But never having seen a safety-pin before, he was surprised when it sprung open as he fiddled with it. As ever, his entrepreneurial mind instantly saw its potential. 'Interesting device,' he muttered as he turned towards the Doctor. 'Where did you get this?'

'I'll tell you later.' He held up his cuffs. 'Just release me from these.'

Mace straightened the pin, inserted it into one of the locks and started to work it around.

'Where did you learn to pick locks?' said Tegan.

Mace cleared his throat. 'I once knew a French acrobat. A charming man... although he couldn't tumble very well... Yet his skill with a piece of bent wire was phenomenal.' Steel rasped against steel as the actor continued to poke around inside the lock. 'Fortunately, he taught me his skill during the period of our acquaintanceship, which has enabled me to extricate my fee from the strongbox of more than one disreputable theatre owner.'

Suddenly there was a click and the cuff fell open.

'*Voilà!*'

'Well done,' said the Doctor, relieved that Mace's skill, unlike his courage in adversity, wasn't all in his imagination.

Quickly Richard Mace freed the Doctor of the second cuff and then started on the lock of the door.

'Wouldn't it be quicker if you used your sonic screwdriver?' said Tegan.

The Doctor pointed at the twisted lump of metal.

'Then what about the pistol?' indicating Mace's flintlock.

'It would be heard,' said Mace, continuing to work on the lock.

'Can't you risk it?' Tegan was insistent.

'I'm nearly there!'

Tegan crossed to the door and peered over Mace's shoulder. 'It's impossible to pick a lock with a safety-pin.'

'I released the Doctor.'

Tegan was becoming annoyed that they were wasting time. 'Yes, but they were handcuffs. I'm talking about a door lock.'

Tegan picked up the pistol and handed it to the Doctor, who checked that it hadn't been damaged when dropped.

'For all we know, the Terileptil and the android have cleared off,' she appealed to the Doctor. 'We can't afford to give them any more time than is absolutely necessary.'

'You're right!'

The Doctor snapped closed the flash-pan cover. 'Stand back!' he said.

'Five seconds more,' demanded Mace.

The Doctor cocked the pistol as the actor continued to waggle the pin about in the lock.

'Stand back please.'

Reluctantly Mace moved away from the door as the Doctor took careful aim and fired. The flintlock kicked hard against the Doctor's grip as it exploded loudly, its shot ripping through the planking of the door just above the lock.

'You missed!' screamed Mace. 'You wasted our only shot.'

The Doctor confidently blew down the barrel of the pistol Western-style. 'I never miss,' he said calmly.

Mace rushed to the door and pointed. 'There is the lock,' he insisted. 'And there is your shot.' He fanned out his fingers and placed them so that they touched both the lock and the bullet-hole. 'A full span separates them!'

Concerned, Tegan looked at the Doctor. This time the actor wasn't exaggerating.

'Try the door.' The Doctor was still calm.

Richard Mace fell on the handle and turned it. To his amazement, the door opened.

'You see,' said the Doctor smugly.

Tegan looked relieved.

'Impossible.' Mace rubbed the stubble on his chin, unable to believe it.

'Let's go,' ordered the Doctor, as he and Tegan moved quickly out of the room. 'That shot might have been heard.'

Mace continued to stare at the door shaking his head. 'Impossible,' he muttered. 'I must have picked it. That's the only explanation.'

Such was Mace's confused state of mind that for a while he blindly followed Tegan and the Doctor along the dark passageway, before realising they were heading in the wrong direction.

'Isn't this the way to the cellar?' he said.

'That's right,' said the Doctor.

The portly actor slid to a halt as the Doctor arrived at the cellar door. 'I am not going down there!' he said in a loud, theatrical whisper. 'That way lies death!'

'Wherever we go is death. Have you forgotten already?'

The actor looked puzzled. 'What do you mean?'

'Do you recall what the Terileptil said before you were fitted with a control bracelet?'

He shook his head.

'The Terileptil is about to release thousands of highly infected rats, carrying a genetically re-engineered plague virus.'

Mace looked confused, but Tegan was stunned. 'Can he do that?' she said.

'He has the knowledge. And even if he lacks the skill, his android could do it for him.'

'You keep using words I do not understand,' said Mace. 'What is genetics?'

'The words don't matter at the moment, only the Terileptil's intention. He wants to rid the planet of its native species. And that includes you,' he said, pointing at Mace. 'That's why we must try and stop him.'

Without waiting for comment, the Doctor silently eased the cellar door open and peered inside. The room was deserted. Quickly he made his way down the steps and across to where the energy barrier was and started to examine the walls.

Tegan and Mace followed reluctantly.

'Where's the entrance to the Terileptil's laboratory?' said Tegan gazing around.

'It's here somewhere,' said the Doctor, starting to move the large, empty ampoule-carrying cases.

'What are you looking for?' asked Tegan.

'The opening mechanism for the energy barrier.'

'Is this it?' she said, removing a stiff, dusty sheepskin from a nail and revealing a small triangular box.

'Press it and see.'

She did, but all that happened was that a light flashed briefly.

'A master control is over-riding the switch.'

Tegan pressed the box again. 'Do you think you can find a way round it?'

'I can try.'

Borrowing the flintlock from Mace, the Doctor started to attack the box with the butt of the gun.

'While I'm doing this, stack some boxes either side of where the opening should be.'

'Now what?' said Tegan.

The Doctor hammered away at the casing. 'If the master over-ride is in operation, it means there is still somebody in the lab.'

The colour drained from Richard Mace's face. 'That is not good news,' he said.

Speedily Tegan and Mace stacked the empty ampoule boxes as instructed, while the Doctor, the casing round the switch now removed, started to fiddle with its internal circuitry.

Inside the laboratory, the miller sat in the Leader's chair oblivious of what was happening.

Although he was still under the influence of the control bracelet, this had in no way affected his appetite, as the feast spread out before him proved.

The miller belched as he refilled his tankard. Then the energy barrier suddenly disappeared. Startled, he slowly got to his feet and, with one eye on the opening the barrier had been concealing, pressed the energising switch. Nothing happened. He repeated his action, but still the opening remained.

Cautiously, he picked up his pistol, cocked it and moved towards the doorway. On seeing the boxes stacked either side of the opening, he paused.

'Who's there?' he called.

There was no reply.

He moved warily into the cellar, forced to pass between the piles of boxes. Suddenly Tegan bobbed up from behind the bench at the end of the cellar. 'Good day!' she said cheekily.

The miller levelled his pistol, but just before he fired, the boxes came cascading down on top of him. Stunned by the weight of them, he fell to the ground, his pistol discharging harmlessly as it hit the floor.

Instantly, the Doctor was amongst the boxes searching for the miller.

'Is he all right?' said Tegan, emerging from behind her bench.

The Doctor disconnected the powerpack and felt the miller's pulse. 'Just stunned,' he said.

Mace raised his arms in triumph. 'You were magnificent,' he said effusively to Tegan.

'You didn't do too badly yourself.'

Having checked the miller could breathe freely, the Doctor stood up. 'We should save the self-congratulations until later.'

'The house is ours! We are victorious!' chanted Mace.

The Doctor crossed to the opening and entered the laboratory. 'We haven't won anything yet.'

'What do you mean, Doctor?'

'The Terileptil and the android have gone. They're still free to carry out their plan!' The Doctor looked around the laboratory. 'And we don't have any idea where they are!'

Chapter 10

With the light almost gone, the warm breeze had turned to a chilly wind. Adric, who was feeling cold and dejected, slowly pushed his way through the thick foliage, unable to understand why the villagers had chosen such a tortuous route to wherever they were now taking him. As he paused to untwine himself from a particularly thorny bush, the villager ahead of him stumbled and fell.

'This is ridiculous,' shouted Adric. 'Why don't you use the path?'

'The path is dangerous,' grunted one of the masked men, 'especially at night.'

Adric watched as the man who had tripped over got to his feet and inspected his bruised knee. 'Can't you at least light a torch?' he protested. 'The next person who falls over may not be so lucky.'

'Walk on, lad!' snapped an impatient voice.

Adric obeyed, forcing his way through the undergrowth. 'I don't understand. Why is the path so dangerous?'

'Things...' muttered one of the villagers cryptically.

'What sort of things?'

'Things that come out at night.'

Adric looked at the masked man. 'Creatures?'

'No, boy. Evil things.'

Adric was still puzzled. From listening to Tegan talk about Earth, he had gained the impression that the planet was relatively free of danger. And that even the larger, potentially more hostile animals, if left alone, were happy to go about their own business.

Although Adric continued to ask questions, the villagers were not very forthcoming about the nature of the 'things'.

Eventually the party emerged in a clearing where several paths met. Adric recognised the place, having passed it earlier that day—they were in fact but a few minutes' walk from the TARDIS, exactly where he had been caught all those hours ago. He looked at the tired villagers and considered, with it being so dark, whether he could make a break for it, and if he did, how much effort they would put into catching him.

As Adric pondered, he noticed, at the same moment one of the villagers did, what appeared to be an enormous firefly drifting along the path ahead of them.

'Run, lads!' a villager shouted. 'Run for your lives!'

Screaming, the villagers fled into the forest in a state of self-induced panic.

Finding himself unexpectedly free, Adric crouched behind a thick bush and waited to see what had upset them so much. As the light grew nearer, he could see that it was the luminous death's-head mask the android was still wearing.

Adric waited, allowing the robot to pass before cautiously relinquishing the cover of the bush and following.

Although it was now quite dark, Adric had little trouble in keeping up, even though the android changed direction several times. If he hadn't been so pleased with himself, Adric might have realised that the robot had made every effort to ensure the boy did not lose track of him.

The Doctor stood before the Terileptil's computer examining the controls.

'Now what do we do?' said Tegan.

'Look around,' the Doctor said distractedly. 'See what there is.'

Tegan flicked through a computer print-out.

'You think he'll have left a forwarding address?'

The Doctor didn't reply, having become engrossed in studying the machinery before him.

Tegan and Mace searched the room as thoroughly as they could, but all the paper they found was either covered in Terileptilian script or mathematical formulae, none of which they could understand.

The Doctor slowly moved along the computer switchboard to the control-bracelet panel.

'You know,' he said, 'I didn't realise the Terileptils were so technologically advanced.'

'I'm pleased you're impressed,' muttered Tegan.

After carefully examining the control panel, the Doctor began to manipulate a row of needle-like levers. This done, he then removed the casing of the panel and studied the banks of printed circuits inside. After a moment's thought, he removed one. 'Let me see them replace that in a hurry,' he said smiling.

'What have you done?' said Tegan crossing to examine the Doctor's work.

'Made the control panel inoperable,' and he slipped the circuit into his pocket.

'But we still don't know where the Terileptil has gone.'

'We must keep looking.'

'For what?' Tegan was beginning to get annoyed with the Doctor's vagueness.

'I'm not sure... until we find it.'

*

With work completed on the sonic booster, all that remained was to test it.

Nyssa entered the console room and switched on the power. For a moment, she stood listening to the hum of electricity, as it surged along the heavy cable. Without first having her work inspected by the Doctor, she was concerned at having to test the booster inside the TARDIS. In theory she knew the machine would work, but if it wasn't adjusted properly, such was its concentrated power, it could quite easily destroy the time machine.

Wishing the Doctor would hurry up, Nyssa looked at the scanner-screen, but could see very little. She then fiddled with the light-intensity control and the picture improved, showing Adric hurriedly entering the clearing where the TARDIS stood. He looked worried, as in fact he was, by the android's sudden disappearance. He was concerned that the robot had discovered he was being followed and had taken evasive action.

Adric increased speed. As he got nearer, the door of the time machine opened and Nyssa stepped out waving. Pleased to see her, he smiled and returned the wave. But his expression turned to one of horror when he saw the android appear at the side of the TARDIS.

'Look out!' screamed Adric.

Nyssa turned and fled into the TARDIS, attempting to close the doors, but the android was already on top of her.

Adric sped across the remaining distance and bravely jumped onto the robot's back, but once again, he was flicked effortlessly away. Stunned by the fall, the boy lay motionless on the ground.

The android paused as he entered the console room, his defence mechanisms alerted by the presence of high technology that was not of Terileptil design.

Although he had caught a glimpse of Nyssa, as she disappeared into the corridor, he could not follow until he had checked that it was safe to do so. This he proceeded to do.

Nyssa crouched at the side of the sonic booster and slipped on a pair of ear-mufflers. Stealthily, she set the booster's slide control on tick-over then switched on the power. The machine quietly started to hum.

She then scrambled across the floor and eased her bed from the wall. This was to be her bolt-hole after the booster was switched to full power. This, she thought, is where I will be triumphant... or die.

The android moved along the corridor towards Nyssa's room, scanning the way ahead. He paused as his attention fixed on the heavy duty cable running along the floor, his sensors indicating a flow of power.

Nyssa repositioned herself by the booster just as the shadow of the android fell across the floor outside the door. She froze in terror, hardly daring to breathe, her hand poised on the booster control.

A moment passed before the android cautiously moved into the doorway. Instantly Nyssa hit the slide control on the booster and the machine screamed into life, a narrow, highly concentrated beam of ultra-sonic sound striking the robot in the chest. Quickly she locked off the control and started to scramble towards her refuge. The android fired, catching the booster a glancing blow and sending her tumbling across the floor. Although unhurt, Nyssa lay where she fell, pretending to be dead. The android fired again, and although scoring a direct hit, the booster continued angrily to roar and scream, its sonic beam tearing into him. Unable to advance, because of the beam's resistance, he was forced to stand his ground and continue to fire. But his power supply was dangerously low.

Suddenly he stumbled as the room began to vibrate. The mirror on Nyssa's dressing table split, then shattered. Ornaments and loose furnishings danced and jigged about, some of them tumbling from their shelves.

The android continued to fire, his aim now less accurate. Again he wobbled badly, as though the strength had been drained from his legs. Nyssa half opened an eye and saw that wisps of smoke were drifting from the android's left knee and that he was having to support himself against the door frame.

The booster continued its relentless pounding. Desperate to relieve the onslaught, the robot fired at the power cable, causing its casing to burst into flames. He fired again, but still the booster did its work.

Smoke was now pouring from both the android's legs as he attempted to drag himself out of the room. Again he wobbled, this time almost overbalancing.

In one last frantic attempt, the robot fired at the booster, but his power was virtually exhausted and the beam fell short, scorching the floor.

Even though she was wearing tightly fitting ear-mufflers, Nyssa was still able to hear the scream of the booster. Suddenly it was joined by another high-pitched note. She opened her eyes and saw that the android's face had started to dissolve. A moment later, he exploded, showering the room with burning debris.

Quickly, Nyssa jumped to her feet and ran to the booster, but was unable to switch it off, the control having been damaged by the android's high-energy beam. She continued to struggle, but the sliding switch would not budge. The sonic beam that had so effectively destroyed the robot was now beginning to attack the structure of the TARDIS.

Nyssa began to panic. She abandoned the switch and worked on the clamp which was holding the cable to the booster. Even that proved an enormous struggle, but at last it came away and the machine fell silent. Nyssa removed her ear-mufflers and quickly ran into the corridor, broke open a locker, removed a fire-extinguisher and sped back to her room where she attacked the burning cable.

When the fire was out, she collapsed onto her bed exhausted. Although she had won, she felt neither elated nor triumphant.

The crunch of footsteps in the corridor announced the arrival of Adric, who had regained consciousness after his fall.

'Nyssa!' he said delightedly, rubbing his head as he entered the room. 'You did it! You destroyed the android.'

'I did it,' she said quietly.

Such was her lack of enthusiasm, Adric feared she had been hurt. 'Are you all right?'

'I'm fine. Just a little sad... it was such a magnificent machine.'

Adric was amazed. 'That machine tried to kill you!'

'It was a slave. It was only doing what it was told.'

Nyssa stood up and started to brush the dust from her tunic. 'I think we should check to see how much damage has been done to the TARDIS.'

Unable to comprehend why Nyssa should be so depressed, he followed her into the corridor. 'What about the Doctor and Tegan?' he said as they entered the console room.

'Where do you think we should start looking?' said Nyssa as she examined the console.

Adric felt the bump on his head again. It was beginning to throb. 'Tegan must still be at the house. And with that thing destroyed,' he said, indicating a piece of the android which had been blown into the console room, 'it's safe to go back there now.'

Nyssa pointed at the scanner.

'It's dark. Aren't you forgetting the woods are full of your friendly villagers?' She looked pointedly at Adric. 'I would have thought you'd had enough of their company for one day.' Nyssa continued to move around the console removing fragments of metal and examining the switching mechanisms for damage.

Adric watched. He knew what he was about to say would not meet with her approval. 'There is a fast way of getting to the house,' he said quietly. 'We could go in the TARDIS.'

Nyssa looked up, her face flushed with anger. 'No!' she shouted. 'If you move this ship, we could finish up anywhere.'

'And if we don't,' he said solemnly, 'the Doctor and Tegan could finish up dead.'

132

Chapter 11

At the manor house the Doctor examined the heavy lock on the front door.

'Well?' said Tegan.

He shrugged. 'Without the sonic screwdriver, there's little I can do.'

'Maybe our actor friend could pick it.'

The Doctor stood up. 'Not this time... We'll have to use the window.'

Quickly they made their way back into the main hall. As the Doctor tried the window, Richard Mace appeared at the landing door, loaded down with weapons and flasks of gunpowder.

Tegan was amazed. 'Where did you find those?'

'In a cupboard on the landing,' said Mace, somewhat embarrassed, 'I felt that as the owners are no longer of this world, they wouldn't mind a poor thespian borrowing them.'

The Doctor smiled to himself as he struggled to open the window.

'Is that the way you propose to leave this building?' Mace asked.

'The main door's locked,' said Tegan.

Mace waved a hand over his portly frame, now made even larger by an array of pistols protruding from his waistband. 'I would never get through.'

'You might if you abandoned some of that junk,' said Tegan tartly.

'Junk!' screamed Mace theatrically. 'This, madam, is our insurance!'

The Doctor jumped down from the sill. 'You can stop arguing. None of us will be able to get through the window. It's been sealed.'

Mace held up one of the powder flasks draped across his broad chest and said, 'I could blow out the main lock.'

'It would be quicker and safer to find the back door,' said the Doctor, making for the landing.

Suddenly they heard the familiar sound of the TARDIS.

Mace unshouldered his musket. 'What's that?' he said, ready to fire his weapon.

The Doctor smiled. 'It's all right. It's help, if we're lucky.'

But something was wrong. The TARDIS had almost materialised when it started to fade again.

'What's wrong?' said Tegan.

'I don't know.' The Time Lord looked worried.

'What's this?' said Mace, watching the fading blue shadow in amazement.

The Doctor and Tegan exchanged worried glances.

'It may be the only glimpse you'll get of my TARDIS,' the Doctor said quietly.

Inside the TARDIS, some very strange noises were coming from the console.

Although she felt on the verge of hysteria, Nyssa said, 'We must try and stay calm.'

The TARDIS creaked and lurched. Nyssa looked around the console room, worried that it might be about to break up.

'I should never have allowed you to talk me into moving the TARDIS.'

Adric flicked more switches, which only seemed to aggravate the instability of the time machine.

'Now what are you doing?' shouted Nyssa.

Suddenly the oscillating time rotor jammed, causing the TARDIS to buck and rock even more violently.

'You realise,' shouted Nyssa, 'that the TARDIS could have been damaged during the fight.' As though to confirm that this was the case, the TARDIS groaned like an enormous prehistorical animal in distress. 'We must try and think what the Doctor would do,' said Nyssa desperately.

'There's only one thing he ever does in situations like this,' said Adric, lifting his hand and delivering the console a hefty thump.

'Brilliant,' said Nyssa without enthusiasm.

But as she spoke, the time rotor began to oscillate and the TARDIS smoothly began to materialise.

Anxiously, they watched as the TARDIS took solid form.

'Shouldn't we hide?' said Tegan urgently. 'The android could be at the helm.'

The Doctor shook his head. 'He would have made a far better job of it.'

Slowly the door of the time machine opened and Adric popped his head out. 'Doctor!' he said as he emerged. 'Tegan!' Adric's face bloomed. 'You're safe. You're all safe.' He shook Richard Mace's hands.

'So you made it at last,' said the Doctor sourly.

Tegan looked sharply at the Time Lord. 'Come on, be grateful,' she said. 'If nothing else it's saved us a long walk.'

With more pomposity .than he intended, the Doctor said, 'I like long walks,' and disappeared into the TARDIS.

'Well, I'm pleased to see you,' said Tegan, smiling broadly.

'And I, too, lad.'

The Doctor interrupted their greetings and urged them to hurry.

'Where's the Terileptil?' asked Adric.

Tegan shrugged. 'I don't know.'

The Doctor stood in the doorway of Tegan and Nyssa's room and surveyed the wreckage. 'Well done,' he said, as Nyssa came to join him. 'You did well.'

Nyssa smiled sadly as she looked at the shattered remains.

'I knew the sonic booster would work in theory,' he continued, 'but...' he shrugged '...in practice—that's something else. You were lucky.'

Horrified, Nyssa stared open-mouthed at the Doctor, as he returned to the console room, where Mace gazed about him in awe. Yet another experience no one would believe: a box larger inside than out. A magician's delight!

The Doctor flicked some switches on the console and the time rotor started oscillating.

'Where are we going?' asked Tegan.

The Doctor tapped the console absent-mindedly. 'In search of the Terileptil.'

'Do you know where he is?'

'Not yet.'

*

137

The miller's wagon rattled noisily along the cobbled street. The city stank of death, with chalk crosses hastily scrawled on the doors of many of its houses, indicating the huge number of plague-victims.

With difficulty, the Terileptil manoeuvred the horse into a narrow side lane. Somewhere in the distance a woman could be heard sobbing and, like some bizarre descant to the crying, a cat screeched in agony.

The Leader pulled hard on the reins and with a loud whinny, the horse came to a halt outside a bakery. Wheezing from the lack of Soliton gas, he slowly climbed down from the box of the wagon and entered the building.

Inside, the wood-burning fires of the ovens roared and crackled, and cast a red glow around the room. Adjusting his cloak to protect his head from the heat, the Leader moved quickly past them and into the shadows, disappearing through a low, narrow door.

He shut the door behind him and leaned against it for a moment, staring ahead at the Soliton machine which was standing in the middle of the floor. Gratefully he inhaled the room's atmosphere.

Stacked along one side of the small room were piles of logs used to fuel the ovens. Around the remaining walls, covering every available space, were hundreds of cages full of black rats. The sight was a sad one, as each rat squeaked pitiably, as though aware of their mission and destiny.

Revived by the Soliton in the air, the Leader moved further into the room, his feet scuffling across the reed-covered floor, and the two remaining Terileptils emerged from the shadows to greet him. Suddenly the air was electric with excitement. They were within reach of their goal. Soon they would be rid of the Earthlings!

The TARDIS hovered over London. On the scanner-screen the Doctor and his party stared at a view of the medieval city beneath them. Suddenly a thin white line appeared and began to travel vertically across the screen.

'Doctor. Will you please tell us why you're doing this?' said Tegan, feeling completely frustrated by his refusal to explain his plan.

'Wait and see!'

Quickly the Doctor pressed several switches on the console and the TARDIS repositioned itself in the night sky. The view on the screen was now of old London Bridge and the surrounding area.

The Doctor operated a lever and the scan-line appeared again and slowly travelled across the screen. As it scanned Southwark, the line wobbled slightly, the distortion growing greater as it reached London Bridge. Suddenly, as the line hit a point on the north side of the Thames, it folded into a triangle and started to flash over a fixed point.

'That's it!' The Doctor was delighted.

Tegan frowned. 'Well, what is it?'

'The Terileptil base!'

Adric checked a dial on the console. 'There's certainly something there.'

The Doctor operated the lever and the section of London was rescanned. This time the blip was larger.

'Absolutely no doubt,' he said.

Tegan was beginning to fume. 'Please tell me what you've found.'

'An electrical emission from a piece of highly sophisticated equipment,' the Doctor said, smiling. 'Not something you would expect to find on seventeenth-century Earth!'

He operated the TARDIS's controls and the time machine materialised near the miller's horse as a clock in the distance struck midnight.

Quickly the Doctor and party emerged into the street, Mace still clutching his musket.

'That's an old friend,' said Nyssa pointing at the wagon.

'Indeed,' muttered the Doctor, crossing to it.

The horse snorted, as though in greeting.

'But where are the Terileptils?' mused Adric. 'They could be anywhere.'

The Doctor pointed at the bakery. 'A miller's wagon outside a bakery,' he said, looking at the boy. 'Where else could the driver be. Come on.'

The party cautiously moved to the darkened entrance and the Doctor tried the door. It was not locked. Silently he eased it open and the group entered, to be greeted by a wall of heat from the ovens. Mace cocked his musket.

'Where are they?' whispered Nyssa.

The Doctor shrugged, looking around. 'We need a torch!' he said.

Instantly Mace rummaged inside his tunic and removed a tinder box. In less time than it takes to light a modern match, he had opened the box, struck steel against flint and ignited a small amount of tinder. Quickly he moved to one of the ovens, and lit a bunch of rush tapers. But as he handed the burning torch to the Doctor, Adric walked into a small stool, sending it crashing across the floor. The party froze, listening.

Silence.

Mace returned the tinder box to his tunic and picked up his musket. As he did so, the Doctor noticed the small door at the back of the oven room, and silently walked over to it.

'Do we go in there?' whispered Tegan, pointing at the door.

The Doctor nodded.

Mace raised his musket to the firing position as the Doctor took a deep breath and quickly pushed it open.

Seated at a desk in the middle of the room was the Terileptil Leader, pen in hand, writing.

'Good evening,' said the Doctor, as jauntily as his apprehension would allow.

'Welcome, Doctor,' the Leader said calmly, placing his pen on the table and rising.

The Doctor moved a little way into the room, Mace at his shoulder.

'You appear to be expecting me,' said the Doctor.

'I was expecting my android. But if you've brought the TARDIS here, so be it.' The Leader's pleasantness was beginning to make the Doctor feel distinctly uneasy. 'Please come in,' he said, beckoning with a webbed hand. 'But first put away your gun.'

'You jest, sir!' said the actor indignantly.

The Leader indicated his own high-energy-beam weapon on the table before him. 'I mean you no harm.'

Cautiously, the Doctor and Mace moved a little further into the room. No sooner had they advanced than one of the Terileptils positioned behind the door seized the barrel of Mace's gun and the other grabbed the Doctor, causing him to drop the flaming taper, which ignited the dry reeds on the floor.

Instead of relinquishing his hold of the weapon, Mace stubbornly clung on as he was swung around. As the muzzle of the weapon came in line with the alien's middle, the actor squeezed the trigger and the reptile collapsed.

But Mace wasn't out of trouble yet. Such was the recoil from the gun, that it sent him spinning, out of control across the room, and into the arms of the Leader. The force of impact caused Terileptil, actor, table and high-energy-beam weapon to go tumbling to the ground.

Meanwhile the Doctor continued to struggle with the second Terileptil, but was seriously outmatched in weight and size, and the Time Lord was soon in trouble. Using his last reserves of strength, the Doctor delivered a massive blow to his attacker's stomach, which sent the reptile staggering backwards.

Seeing her chance, Tegan rushed into the room, picked up the musket Mace had dropped and started to beat the winded Terileptil about the body.

The Doctor stood dazed in the middle of the room, feeling sick and dizzy, as Mace continued to struggle frantically, trying to free himself from the Leader's grip.

Suddenly the burning reeds flared up and ignited the store of logs. Adric and Nyssa snatched up sacks and attempted to stamp out the spreading blaze.

With the Doctor's attacker taken care of, Tegan turned her attention to helping Mace. Savagely she struck out at the Leader and caught him a nasty blow on the head.

As the Leader let out a loud, shrill scream of pain, the room was filled with a second sound, which instantly brought the Doctor out of his daze. 'Out of here!' he shouted, seeing that the Leader's gun was now on fire. 'Quickly!'

'But the flames,' shouted Adric. 'We must try and put the fire out.'

'There isn't time,' bellowed the Doctor. 'The powerpack in that gun is about to explode.'

The Doctor and his companions fled from the room as flames began to embrace the Soliton machine. The Leader grunted loudly as they departed and began to regain consciousness. The other Terileptils were silent and still: one dead from Mace's musketball—the other stunned from Tegan's attack. As the Leader looked around the burning room, he was filled with despair. He had lost. And soon, he realised, he would be dead.

The fire spread even more quickly as the Soliton machine exploded, bringing down the bakery roof.

Out in the smoke-filled street, Nyssa shouted above the noise, 'Shouldn't we try and help the Terileptils?'

There was a secondary explosion.

'It's too late,' said the Doctor.

As he spoke, Mace began to lead the miller's horse away from the burning building. 'Wait!' shouted the Doctor as he tugged at the tarpaulin covering the back of the wagon, and revealed further ampoule boxes. 'Everything into the flames!' he said, as he snatched up several containers.

Quickly the others helped, throwing the boxes of ampoules deep into the flames. As they worked, a night watchman arrived.

'Fetch a squirter!' ordered Mace. 'Arouse the street.'

The confused man ran off to do as instructed.

With the ampoule boxes destroyed, Mace slapped the horse's rump and the animal trotted off to safety.

'We must go,' said the Doctor. 'Our presence here would raise too many awkward questions.' Mace nodded that he understood, as the Doctor's companions entered the TARDIS. 'Can I drop you anywhere?' the Doctor added.

Mace looked at the burning building behind him and smiled. 'Your pace of life is a little too fast for me, sir,' he said. 'I shall stay and fight the fire.'

'Goodbye,' said the Doctor.

Both men shook hands, a little sad that their departure was so sudden and abrupt.

'Wait!' said the Doctor, producing the printed circuit he had removed from the control panel. 'A keepsake,' he said, handing it to the actor. 'Goodbye and good luck.'

Richard Mace gave a final wave as the Doctor entered the TARDIS and closed the door.

'Shouldn't we help put out the fire?' said Tegan. 'We are partly responsible.'

The Doctor started to set the co-ordinates on the console.

'I have a sneaking feeling,' he said with a wry smile, 'this fire should be allowed to run its course.'

'What do you mean?' Tegan was puzzled.

The Doctor grinned. 'I'll tell you one day.'

Watched by Mace, the TARDIS dematerialised. On the wall behind the fading time-machine was a plate bearing the name of the road: Pudding Lane.

About the Author

Eric Saward

Born in 1944, Eric Saward worked initially as an estate agent. After a short period living in Holland, Saward returned to Britain and worked in various roles within the publishing industry, and as a sales assistant in a bookshop. From this he moved into teaching and while working as an English teacher had his radio drama script *The Fall and Fall of David Moore* accepted.

Giving up teaching in order to write full-time, Saward took various other jobs to supplement his income, including working in theatre.

Recommended to *Doctor Who*'s script editor Christopher H. Bidmead because of the quality of his radio work, Saward was commissioned to write *The Visitation* for Peter Davison's first season as the Doctor. On the strength of this script, Saward was appointed Bidmead's successor as the programme's script editor.

Since leaving *Doctor Who* in 1986, Saward has continued to work as a freelance writer.

Here are details of other exciting Doctor Who *titles from BBC Books:*

DOCTOR WHO AND THE WEB OF FEAR
Terrance Dicks   £6.99
ISBN 978 1 785 94036 1   **A Second Doctor Adventure**

*With a sudden, shattering roar the Yeti smashed down its arm
in a savage blow . . .*

The TARDIS is engulfed by a mysterious web-like substance
in space. Breaking free, the Doctor and his companions
Jamie and Victoria land in the London Underground
system. But a creeping killer mist has meant that London
has been evacuated. The Great Intelligence is back – and
its robot Yeti are roaming the streets and the underground
tunnels.

The Doctor, Jamie, and Victoria team up with an army
unit working with their old friend Professor Travers to
combat the menace. The group's new commanding officer is
Colonel Lethbridge-Stewart – who the Doctor will come to
know far better in the years ahead.

As the Doctor begins to wonder if the Great Intelligence
has planned everything simply to trap him, he also realises
that someone in the group must be working for the
Intelligence. With time running out, the Doctor and his
friends realise they can trust no one . . .

*This novel features the Second Doctor as played by Patrick
Troughton with his companions Jamie and Victoria. It is a
novelisation of the TV story by Mervyn Haisman and Henry
Lincoln first broadcast in February–March 1968.*

DOCTOR WHO AND THE GENESIS OF THE DALEKS
Terrance Dicks   £6.99
ISBN 978 1 785 94038 5   A Fourth Doctor Adventure

'Alien,' croaked the Dalek suddenly. *'Exterminate . . . exterminate . . . exterminate!'* Slowly the gun stick raised until it was pointing straight at the Doctor.

The Time Lords have a mission for the Doctor. Together with Sarah and Harry, he finds himself stranded on the war-torn planet Skaro where the conflict between the Thals and the Kaleds has been raging for a thousand years. Chemical and biological weapons have started a cycle of mutation among the planet's inhabitants that cannot be stopped. But Kaled scientist Davros has perfected a life support system and travel machine for the creature – the Dalek.

The Doctor's mission is to stop the creation of the Daleks, or perhaps affect their development so they evolve into less aggressive creatures.

Captured by the Kaleds, the Doctor and Harry meet the first prototype Dalek. Out in the wastelands, Sarah is attacked by hideous mutated creatures and taken prisoner by the Thals. With Davros's plans to destroy the Thals and to wipe out any dissenters among his own ranks in progress, is the Doctor already too late?

This novel features the Fourth Doctor as played by Tom Baker with his companions Sarah Jane Smith and Harry Sullivan. It is a novelisation of the TV story by Terry Nation first broadcast in March–April 1975.